Belle

Belle

Treasure Hernandez

www.urbanbooks.net

Urban Books, LLC
300 Farmingdale Road, NY-Route 109
Farmingdale, NY 11735

ISBN 13: 978-1-64556-161-3
ISBN 10: 1-64556-161-5

First Mass Market Printing April 2021
First Trade Paperback Printing November 2019
Printed in the United States of America

10 9 8 7 6 5 4 3 2 1

This is a work of fiction. Any references or similarities to actual events, real people, living or dead, or to real locales are intended to give the novel a sense of reality. Any similarity in other names, characters, places, and incidents is entirely coincidental.

Distributed by Kensington Publishing Corp.
Submit Orders to:
Customer Service
400 Hahn Road
Westminster, MD 21157-4627
Phone: 1-800-733-3000
Fax: 1-800-659-2436

Belle

Treasure Hernandez

Integrity is the lifeblood of democracy.
Deceit is a poison in its veins.

—Edward Kennedy

Prologue

Lucas Dubois sat staring at the screen of his laptop computer, and suddenly it felt as if his tie were choking him. Or maybe it was that the contents on the screen were making it hard for the brandy he was sipping to go down. He loosened the royal blue Stefano Ricci tie, but the lump in his throat didn't go anywhere. The time was two in the morning, and Lucas sat alone at the long marble island in the large kitchen of his home. He'd arrived an hour prior, and instead of going to his room and getting into bed with his wife, he'd decided to pop in the small USB drive that had been placed anonymously on his desk. He couldn't believe what he was looking at. The only thought running through his mind was, how could he have been so stupid?

"Shit," he said and rubbed his face with the large palm of his hand. "Shit!"

He caught himself before he shouted out again. He didn't want to wake his sleeping wife and son. He definitely didn't want his wife to know why he was so upset. Not after everything he'd sacrificed for his business and for them to have the life they had. However, soon she would know. But by then the ball would be back in his court. When he found the USB on his desk, there was also a sticky note attached to it with a phone number inked on it. Grabbing his cellular phone from the pocket of his dress slacks, he dialed that very same number and waited for it to stop ringing.

"I see you got my present," a distorted voice answered after the third ring. "I hope it found you well."

"Yeah," Lucas said. "I found it. Just got finished viewing the file on it."

"Good. Now we can discuss terms, Mr. Dubois. Well, more like numbers. I think two hundred and fifty thousand dollars is a great starting point."

Lucas took another gulp of his brandy before scoffing into the phone. The scoff soon turned into a full-blown laugh. He put the glass down and picked up the USB drive, staring down at it briefly before he spoke again.

"Starting point?" he inquired. "Go fuck yourself."

"What?"

"I said go fuck yourself. I don't think I stuttered."

"Think wisely. If what is on that USB gets out, your entire business will be ruined. Think of your family."

"I am thinking about my family. If I give you two hundred and fifty thousand now, you'll come back. It might not be now, or even in a year. But you'll come back, and you'll keep coming back," Lucas answered, getting up from the island and walking over to the sink. "And because of that, I'm going to put my big-boy pants on and deal with whatever scrutiny this little fiasco comes with. So my answer to you is no. I may lose a lot, more than I want to, but I keep my dignity. And that is worth more to me than even this business. Have a good night . . . whoever you are."

Lucas disconnected the phone and put it back in his pocket. He set the USB drive on the granite countertop and grabbed the meat tenderizer out of the drainer next to the sink. He swung down one good time and destroyed the small black device. All that was left of it were it-ty-bitty pieces. Of course, he knew whoever was black-mailing him would have made plenty of copies by then, but he didn't care. He didn't want it in his house.

After disposing of all the evidence, Lucas powered down his laptop, flipped the kitchen light off, and headed upstairs to get in bed. Maybe it was because of the liquor coursing through his body or because he was so tired that he forgot to arm the home's alarm system.

Upstairs he started to walk down the long hallway toward the master bedroom's closed door, but he paused and turned around. Instead, he headed to the other side of the hallway where the kids' rooms were. Lucas peeked in on his son, Luca, who was sound asleep and, as usual, on top of his comforter, wearing his favorite dinosaur pajamas. Lucas smiled to himself and shook his head. He didn't know what the kid had against being under-neath covers, but with the way his mom was against the thermostat being over seventy-four degrees at night, he needed them. Lucas entered the room and tucked Luca underneath the covers, kissing his forehead before he left almost as quickly as he came.

His next stop was his daughter Belle's room. He opened the door, turned on the light, and smiled. She was away at college, but with as much life as her bedroom had, it was like she was still there with them all. Pictures of herself with friends and posters of her favorite celebrities were sprawled all over her walls. The room smelled of clean linen, Belle's favorite scent, and her bed was neat, which it never would have been had she been home. She was his pride and joy. There was nothing he felt she couldn't do, and he felt in his heart that she would be something great, if she didn't want to take over his business, that was.

He smiled to himself once more before flicking the light back off and shutting the door. The last thing he needed was for her to come home screaming about how someone had been in her room while she'd been gone. The last time that happened, Luca's PlayStation ended up broken, and Lucas wasn't trying to shell out another $400 to replace another one.

As he finally made his way to his master bedroom, he began to unbutton his shirt. He envisioned Taina groaning in her sleep and complaining about how he wreaked of cheap liquor.

"E & J are old friends. They give me the best advice," he would say right before he pulled her close and buried his head in the back of her neck.

Most people couldn't say that they had lucked out and married the love of their life. But Taina was everything and more for him. He felt like a blessed man whenever he made it back home to her. He made a promise to her the day they got married that she wouldn't regret taking his last name, and so far he'd kept that promise.

The door was slightly open, and he smirked to himself. She must have heard him in the hallway. "I always forget that you could hear a mouse's footsteps in your sleep," Lucas said upon entering the room, but he instantly froze when he saw that his wife was still sound asleep.

However, standing over her, wearing a black ski mask, was a man Lucas didn't recognize. He was tall, about six feet, and Lucas didn't like how he was looking at Taina in her sleep. He walked up on the man, preparing to cause damage if need be.

"What are you doing in my house?" he demanded to know in a hushed tone. "Get away from my wife!"

Lucas was so focused on how closely the man in front of him was to the bed that he didn't notice the gun with an attached silencer in his hand. When he finally did, he stopped in his tracks, and the man in the ski mask finally looked his way.

"You should have taken the deal, Lucas," the man said and sighed. "You should have just . . . taken the deal. Now you have to pay."

Fwap!

Lucas hadn't realized that somebody else had come up from behind him until he felt the pain in the back of his head. The blow knocked him to the ground, and when he touched the throbbing point and looked at his fingers, he saw that they were covered in blood. Another man wearing a matching mask had entered the room, and he was holding a gun too.

"Did you really think that you could tell me to fuck myself without consequences?" the first man asked and pointed his gun at Taina's sleeping body. "She's a deep sleeper, isn't she?"

What he didn't know was that she probably had her sleeping plugs in, which she often wore when she had a long day. The man's finger wrapped around the trigger, and Lucas felt fear in the pit of his stomach that he'd never experienced.

"Wait!" Lucas cried, putting his hands up and struggling back to his feet. "I'll give you anything. Whatever you want. You got it. Two hundred and fifty thousand? I'll have it wired to any account you want. Just please don't hurt my family. Please."

The man paused and lowered the gun. He looked back at Lucas, and a smile formed in the mouth of the mask.

"We figured you'd come around," he said, and Lucas took a small breath of relief. "But unfortunately for you, that offer is off the table now. The boss feels that you're more valuable to us dead."

He raised his gun again and shot the sleeping woman in her head without so much as blinking an eye. Lucas's scream filled the room. He tried to leap at the man, but he was too slow. Before he could even lay a hand on him, the same gun that had killed his wife was pointed at the middle of his face.

Pfft! Pfft!

Two shots to the face made him drop like a fly. The second man in the room checked their pulses and nodded when he was sure they were both dead. He stood back up and made a distressed sound.

"You get to have all the fun," he said.

"No worries. You get to do the fun part," the first masked man said and nodded down the hall. "No witnesses, remember."

The second man looked down the hall to where he'd seen a kid sleeping in his bed. He gave his partner a look before walking out of the room and to the kid's bedroom. He stood in the doorway for a second and watched his chest go up and down. He'd kicked the covers off of his body in his sleep, although the house wasn't that warm. The gun in the man's hand rose, aimed at the little boy. As he prepared to tug the trigger, his hand wavered slightly. But that wouldn't stop him from doing what needed to be done.

"Sleep tight, kid . . . forever."

Pfft!

Chapter 1

What we have once enjoyed we can never lose.
All that we love deeply becomes a part of us.
                                                    —Helen Keller

"Sometimes life isn't kind to any of us, and time is limited. We don't know why the Dubois family was taken from this earth so soon. All I can say is the devil is working. You hear me? The devil is working! So in this great time of pain, we ask you, Lord, to wrap your heavenly arms around each and every shoulder in this congregation today. We ask that you catch every tear falling and ease every aching heart. We send a special prayer today to our sister Belle in this tumultuous time. Remind her that through this great loss she still has been granted with the gift of life. . . ."

At that moment, Reverend Ingram's words seemed to run together, and Belle Dubois lost track of what he was saying. She never thought in a million years that she'd be sitting in the front row, staring at the lifeless bodies of her family lying in three caskets. Her mother, her father, and her 7-year-old brother were all gone, just like that. The veil connected to the black hat on her head covered the despair all over her face, but it did nothing to help the aching pain in the pit of her stomach.

Just a week ago, Belle was away and enjoying the college life in Texas. Her parents had just bought her a new all-white 2018 Chevrolet Camaro, and life couldn't get any better. That was, until it got a whole lot worse. Belle had just returned to her dorm room after a night out when she got the call that turned her life upside down.

Her entire family had been murdered in their sleep.

She flew home as fast as she could, but she didn't even remember the trip. Everything after that phone call was a blur, even talking to the detectives in the interrogation room. There was one thing the detective said that rang over and over in her head: *"We think whoever did this was after your father. Your mother and your brother were just casualties in the crossfire."*

Her father, Lucas Dubois, was a very wealthy man and had a heart of gold. Same with her mother. Belle didn't know who would do such a thing to her family. Whoever it was had to have been pretty sick and sadistic to kill a 7-year-old kid.

"Oh, Luca," Belle whispered as she stared at the smallest casket before her. "I love you forever."

Tears ran down her face in a warm stream, and she felt a strong arm wrap around her shoulders. The gesture should have been a comforting one, but when she saw that the arm belonged to her uncle Karan, she pulled away and jumped to her feet. Shooting a glare his way, she gathered her things and stormed out of the church, suddenly needing to be alone. She couldn't take it. Not only had she lost her family, but she'd lost everything else, too.

"Belle!" she heard her aunt Sinthia shout, but it was too late.

Belle couldn't stand it any longer. Even when she was sitting with her back to the entire church, she could feel all eyes on her. She couldn't even grieve in peace. The last five days of her life had been a complete nightmare, and the things she was feeling inside she wouldn't wish on anybody. Once out of the church, she threw the black veil from her face and bent over with her hands on the knees of her black dress. She gasped for air as if she'd just emerged from a pool after being under too long. She didn't care about the air nipping away at her damp cheeks on that cold Nebraska day. All she wanted to do was get as far away as possible from the North Omaha church.

"Belle!"

Belle straightened up and whisked around to see that her aunt Sinthia, Uncle Karan's wife, had followed her outside. Belle returned the concerned look on her aunt's face with a glare of her own.

"Belle! Why did you run out like that?"

"Leave me alone, Sinthia. Go back in there with your crook of a husband!"

"Now you wait a good minute, young lady! You will not speak about your uncle like that, especially on a day like this! I don't think Taina would appreciate you acting this way."

"You mean on the day that he stole everything my father owned?" Belle shouted. When she saw the shocked look on her aunt's face, she scoffed. "Yeah, that's right. I know everything! The lawyer paid me a visit right before I left for the funeral. He told me that my father died before he could finish his will. He also told me that because I am not Lucas Dubois's biological child, I have no right to any of his businesses or his money. Can you guess where all of that plus his assets will go? Can you guess,

Auntie? You. You and your husband. That bastard put our
house on the market yesterday! My family isn't even in
the dirt yet! I have nothing! No home. No family. I have
five hundred dollars to my name because my accounts
have been frozen. So fuck you! Fuck you and your husband. And don't you ever say my mother's name again
if you know what's good for you. After today, neither of
you will ever see me again!"

Belle didn't wait for her to say another word, but even
if she had, no words would come. Sinthia could do nothing but place her hand on her chest and watch Belle storm
off to the only thing she had in the world: her car.

Once the door to the Camaro slammed closed, Belle
angrily hit the steering wheel with her gloved fists.
Snatching the hat from her head, she threw it to the
side and began to scream. She was feeling every human
emotion at one time, and it felt as if she were going to
explode. She was lost, had nowhere to go, and had no
real family to call on.

She'd lost track of how long she was sitting in her vehicle, sobbing and crying, when finally she stopped and
pulled down her visor to get a good look at her face. Her
eyes were puffy and bloodshot.

*"My Belle, my beauty. You will always be the most
beautiful girl in any room you walk in."*

Taina's voice sounded in Belle's head. It was something she'd told her daughter since she was old enough to
walk. She always told Belle that she was a different kind
of gorgeous. Some would even say her beauty was out of
this world. Taina had been very easy on the eyes herself,
but her looks were nothing compared to Belle's. That was
why she gave her the name in the first place.

Although Belle had taken Taina's brown skin and curvy figure, she had other exotic features, and she never knew the origin of them. Taina always claimed to have been slightly wild in college. Therefore, she could never pinpoint who Belle's father was. That meant Taina would never know where her amber eyes, her slightly pointed nose, or the long, fine hair on the top of her head came from. It was something that used to eat away at Belle as a kid, but when Taina married Lucas when Belle was 5 years old, none of that mattered anymore. She finally had a dad to love her and give them the life they deserved. Lucas loved Belle like his own flesh, so it was only fitting that he give his last name to her too.

If Lucas could have seen her now, he would have lifted her chin and said, "Head up, buttercup. The world would love to see you fail. But we are Duboises, and we don't fail."

Belle wiped away the remaining tears on her face and blinked her eyes until her vision was clear. She couldn't believe that God could be so cruel. She didn't want to live in a world without her family. Why couldn't she have been killed too? She looked back at the church. People had started to file out and clear the way for the pallbearers. Belle contemplated going to the gravesite to pay her last respects, but when she started her car, she didn't follow the others.

"I have to get out of here," Belle said to herself.

There was nothing left in Nebraska for her, and it was time to say her final goodbye. She drove in the direction of the interstate, not knowing where her final stop would be. Texas was out of the question. The only reason she'd been there was for school, and she couldn't even imagine going back. She had no destination. She just paid attention to the road and blasted her music so that the faces of her family wouldn't flood her mind. The only time she stopped was to get gas.

When the sun was completely gone and the moon had taken its place, she had arrived in a hick town in Illinois. A sign on the side of the highway said that there was a gas station up ahead called Jim's Fuel, Dine & Go. Something told her to keep going to the next exit, but her gas hand was warning her that if she didn't fill up again soon, she wouldn't make it anywhere. She also really wanted to get out of the funeral clothes she'd had on all day.

She veered off on the exit that led her to Jim's, and she parked at the nearest pump to the door. There were a few trucks and Jeeps parked in front of the station, but mostly there were motorcycles. Checking her surroundings, she saw that all of the roads were dark. Across the street from the gas station was a junkyard that looked as creepy as a cemetery. She could hear old rock and roll songs coming from the building when she stepped out of her car. She popped her trunk with the car remote in her hand and from it got a pair of jeans, a long-sleeved cream shirt, a pair of Chanel boots, and her red bubble coat. She shut the trunk and took a deep breath.

Just get in and get out, she told herself. *You don't know what type of time these white folks are on.*

As she made her way to the front door, she noticed that the majority of the men dining inside had turned their attention to her. The way they were peering at her through the glass was making her uneasy. She pulled the door open, and instantly the smell of grease hit her and reminded her that she couldn't even remember the last time she put something in her stomach. Still, she would take her chances elsewhere.

The place was set up like something she'd seen in a movie. One side was the gas station, where you could get all of the things a person would need for the road, while the other side was set up like a diner from the fifties. The two waitresses even wore blue and white checkered dresses with red aprons. Belle tried not to be bothered by the fact that, besides her, they were the only other women in the building. She pulled two $20 bills out of her pocket and pushed them toward the tall, lanky clerk. His graying blond beard was unkempt, and although the hair on his head was long, there was a shiny bald spot at the top of it. He had all of his teeth, but that didn't say much given that they were all yellow. His name tag read JIM, so naturally Belle assumed that he owned the place.

"Can I put forty on the Camaro out there?" she asked and pointed to her car outside.

"Anything for something as beautiful as you," Jim said and winked. "What you doing out this way by yourself, sugar?"

"Just passing through and needed some gas."

"Well, if I were you, I'd be more cautious about stopping into strange places. This town is full of wolves," he said with a chuckle. Behind Belle, many of the men in the diner began to howl.

Belle glared behind her and was met with even more cringeworthy stares. She clenched her jaw and swallowed the spit in her mouth before turning back toward the clerk.

"I can handle myself," she said.

"Oh! Well, lookee here, fellas, we have a lady here who can handle herself!" Jim shouted to the guests in the diner. They returned his declaration with whistles.

"Where is your bathroom?" Belle asked.

"Down that hallway right there," he said and pointed down a hallway to her left. "Be careful, that knob is a little tricky."

Belle turned before she saw his sly smile or his eyes travel down her entire body. Her feet made their way on the tiled floor to where he'd directed her. When she finally found the bathroom, she flicked the light on and was pleased that it was cleaner than what she expected. Shutting the door behind her, she locked it and began to undress. The music in the diner seemed to grow louder, but she didn't care. All she wanted to do was hurry up and get dressed so she could go pump her gas. Belle had just fastened her jeans and was about to put on her shirt when she heard the knob twist and the door open. Instantly Belle covered herself up and whisked around.

Standing behind her were Jim and two other men from the diner. One was a redhead while one was completely bald. The things they had in common were that they were both big in size and they both wore leather. The redhaired man's eyes went to Belle's cleavage. He licked his lips while the other grinned sinisterly at her.

"I'm not done yet," she said, trying to hide the fear in her voice.

"I warned you about that knob, didn't I, sweetheart?" Jim said. "The lock don't work.

"I said I'm not done yet," Belle repeated.

"I saw the plates on your car," Jim said, ignoring her again. "Nebraska, huh? You're a long way from home. Fellas, what do you say we give this beautiful young thing right here a nice, hearty welcome? Bob, tell me, when's the last time you had some nigger pussy?"

"It's been a while, Jim," the bald man said and watched as Belle backed away from them until her back was on the opposite wall. "But I can't help but wonder if this one here is as sweet as what I remember."

"She looks like she'll be sweeter," the redhaired man said, licking his lips and unbuckling his belt. "There is nothing like a pair of chocolate nipples in your mouth with black pussy around your cock."

"Please," Belle begged, covering herself with one arm and putting the other up in a stop motion. "You don't have to do this."

"Of course we don't have to do it. We want to," Jim said and flicked the lights off.

Belle screamed and tried to fight them off in the dark, but it was no use. They just laughed at her as they fondled her body. She felt a hand cup her crotch while another pulled her breast out of her bra.

"No point in screaming, sugar," she heard Jim say in her ear. "Those sons of bitches out there don't care about what we do to you. They're waiting for their turn."

His breath smelled like whiskey and cigarettes, and at that point Belle was sobbing while the men had their way with her. She felt two different mouths around her nipples at the same time while someone was trying to tug her jeans down. She screamed one last time in hopes that someone in the establishment had a heart.

By the grace of God, the door to the bathroom burst open and the lights flicked back on. "You sick white motherfuckers!" a woman's voice shouted. "Kidd, go get Jay and them! They back here tryin'a rape some girl! Bring the fires!"

The next few moments of Belle's life seemed like a blur. The men on her were pulled off, and she was able to see a young black woman around her age standing there and pointing a gun at them.

"Get out!" she barked at the men, and all but Jim listened.

"Hey, hey! This is my establishment, and you need to get the fuck out of here!" Jim yelled.

The woman sneered, and her eyes traveled to his unbuckled pants. "It's not hard to figure out the kind of shit that goes on here," she said. She aimed her gun at his crotch and fired.

Jim's high-pitched screams were like nails on a chalkboard. He gripped his bleeding penis in his hands as he fell to the ground, yelling in agony. The young woman turned to Belle, who had finished getting dressed, and threw the bubble coat at her.

"Put that on," she instructed, and when Belle did, she took her hand. "Let's go. Stay behind me."

As they walked, the woman kept her gun drawn until they were out of the hallway and far enough away from the bathroom. In the diner, there were two grown black men pointing automatic guns at the guests while another was waiting for the young woman. He was a handsome guy with thick black waves on top of his head. His thick sideburns made way to a well-kept short beard on his face. He looked at the young woman holding Belle's hand and grabbed her by the shoulder.

"You good?" he asked her.

She nodded. "I shot that motherfucker in the dick," she said with a grin. "So yeah, I'm good. She's the one you should be worried about."

"Are you good, *mami?*" he asked, and Belle nodded.

"I didn't get to pump my gas," she said in a low voice.

The guy looked at her with shock in his eyes and then back toward the hallway where Jim was still shrieking in pain. "Those men just tried to hurt you, and all you're worried about is putting gas in your car?"

"Yes," Belle said and pulled her hand free. She turned to the young woman and nodded. "Thank you for saving me. But I have somewhere I have to be."

She moved past the guy and walked out of the gas station to her car. Her hands were shaky as she pumped her gas, half surprised that Jim had even put her money on the pump. When she was done, Belle put the nozzle back on its holder and bent slightly to close the door to the fuel tank of the Camaro. When she stood straight again, the young woman who had saved her was blocking the driver's door.

"You left these," she said and handed Belle the clothes she left behind.

"Thank you. You all should go before they call the police," Belle suggested and went for the door handle, but the woman slid her butt over to block that too.

"I don't think that will be a problem," she said. "None of the cameras in there work. Plus I'm sure they don't want their guilty pleasure to get out in the streets. I have a feeling this isn't the first time this type of thing has happened. With the whole Me Too movement, I doubt they'll want to be under that judging eye."

Belle took in the girl before her. She was casually wearing designer clothes from head to toe. The snake skin YSL bag with the long strap on her shoulder was the exact one Belle had eyed a few weeks ago. She had on an oversized tan cargo coat that went well with the Gucci boots on her feet. Her skin was brown, like Belle's, and she had thick, full lips that pursed in Belle's direction. Her hair was pulled up in a sleek ninja bun, which brought out every feature her face had to offer, such as her bright hazel eyes, long eyelashes, and slender nose.

"What's your name?" Belle asked.

"Aria. Yours?"

"Belle. I just want to thank you, Aria, for saving me from having twenty white dicks shoved inside of me. Now if you please, let me go."

"Where are you going?"

"What?"

"You don't even know, do you?" Aria guessed.

"I do know where I'm going," Belle lied through her teeth.

"Right," Aria said, staring into Belle's pupils. "Who died?"

"H . . . how do you know—"

"Your eyes. You have the eyes of someone who just experienced great sadness, such as a loss. You acting so nonchalant after what just happened, plus seeing my Gs standing there with automatic guns, told me either this has happened to you before, or you're numb from death. I opted for the latter." She shrugged. "Who was it?"

"None of your business."

"All right." Aria moved out of the way so Belle could get in her car. "Just here to help. Oh, and I don't know how far you think you're going to make it with five hundred dollars, but good luck to you. You left this too."

She gave Belle back all the money she had in the world and turned her back on her. Belle watched Aria walk toward what looked to be something like a tour bus. On the side of the bus, it said GENE'S GIRLS, and the guy who had spoken to her earlier was standing next to it, waiting for Aria.

"Wait! Aria!" Belle didn't know what made her call Aria's name. Maybe it was because her words had more than a little truth to them.

"Yes?" Aria stopped and turned back to Belle.

"My entire family."

"Huh?"

"That's who died. My entire family. My mom, my dad, and my little brother. Murdered in their sleep last week. This is all the money I have, and I don't have anywhere to go. All I have is this car and some clothes in the trunk."

"What about your other family?"

"If you can call them that. They're the reason I'm homeless." Belle shrugged. "I was going to college in Texas."

"Why not just go back there?" Aria asked.

Belle shook her head. "I can't go back there," she breathed. "I wouldn't be able to afford tuition. I've never had a job before."

Aria studied Belle for a moment, searching her face for a lie. When she didn't find one, she looked back at the bus and then back to Belle. She held up a finger and jogged toward the guy. They exchanged a few words before he glanced around her at Belle. When he turned back to Aria, he nodded and said something else before disappearing on the bus.

Aria jogged back to Belle and smiled. "You wanna roll with me?"

"Roll where?"

"Does it matter? You don't have anywhere to be. You've already proven that you shouldn't be alone, and I have a way for you to keep some money in your pockets. You down or what? You have about five seconds to decide."

"Okay," Belle's lips said before her mind had fully comprehended what Aria had said. She didn't even think to question what kind of job Aria was putting on the table. All she knew was that she was alone. And them? They had guns, and from the looks of it, they had money, too. She didn't ever again want to feel as helpless as those men made her feel, and for some reason, Aria made her feel safe.

"Okay?" Aria asked to double-check.

"Yeah. Okay."

"Yes! Follow that bus," Aria said, going over to the Camaro's passenger's side.

Once they were both in the car and driving away from the gas station, Belle made sure to follow closely behind the bus as they got back on the highway. Aria was leaned back in her seat, messing with Belle's radio.

"Man, this hick-ass town doesn't have any good radio stations!" she complained.

"You can hook your phone up to the Bluetooth and play whatever song you like if you want," Belle suggested.

"I left my phone on the bus," she replied. "We were only stopping because I wanted some snacks. Which I didn't get because I heard you screaming from the bathroom. I knew something was off about that damn place. Hey, you sure you're okay? I saw what those guys were doing to you and—"

"I'm fine."

"No, you aren't."

"If you know that, then why did you ask?"

"I just wanted to see if you'd talk about it." Aria shrugged. "That's the only way to get past shit. Put it on the table."

"Yeah, well, what they did to me is nothing compared to the pain I feel inside. I'll get over it. I was in college, for crying out loud. I've woken up naked more than once next to a guy I barely knew after a drunk night. I'll live."

"Sounds like you've lived quite the exciting life there, Belle," Aria said, smirking at her.

"Yeah," Belle scoffed. "Hardly. So where are we going?"

"Indianapolis. We have some clients there."

"We?"

"Yeah, me and the other girls."

"Wait, there are other girls?"

"Um, yeah. Why do you think we need a tour bus, silly?" Aria giggled.

"Uh, what do you guys do exactly?"

"You can't tell from my long, acrylic nails or this fat ass draped in designer clothes? I'm an entertainer, girl! An exotic dancer, to be more specific."

"Gene's Girls are strippers?"

"Ah, ah! Exotic dancers," Aria said with a finger in the air.

"Excuse me. Gene's Girls are exotic dancers?"

"Yes, we are. Any problem with that?"

"Not at all," Belle said. "But I've never done that kind of dancing a day in my life. What kind of job would you have me do?"

"You're over twenty-one, right?"

"Yeah. Twenty-three."

"Me too," Aria said, smiling. "All you have to do is put on something alluring—not too much, since you won't be dancing—and welcome the guests into the party. Seeing a face as gorgeous as yours, those thirsty motherfuckers will be lined up at the door to see what else we have to offer. And don't worry, you'll have security standing right next to you, making sure nobody gets out of line."

"The guys with the guns?"

"Ding, ding! Let's just say Gene doesn't play about his merchandise."

"And this Gene, he won't care that you're bringing in a stray?"

"He won't know until we've gotten back to Miami. We're on tour right now and have about five more stops on the road ahead of us. That's a quick li'l band for you every night we do a party."

"A thousand dollars a night?" Belle asked with big eyes.

"Yeah, but don't get too excited. Not to burst your little bubble, but we dancers make about five thousand a party. And if you're fucking the guys, which I could never, you can make double that."

"Five thousand?" Belle almost swerved the car. "Who comes to these parties?"

"Ballers, bosses, celebrities. We were just at one of Blac Youngsta's parties a month ago. That man throws cake, okay?"

"Wow." Belle's voice trailed off as her mind was reeling. "And all I have to do is welcome them?"

"Yes. You'll be the first form of contact for them. Stand there, smile, tell them to have a good night and get paid. If you do good, by the time we get to Miami, Gene might want to make you a permanent part of Gene's Girls."

"I doubt I'll be around that long," Belle said, and Aria gave her a curious side-eye. "But that will be a good way to make some money in the meantime. Until I figure out what my next move is."

"Welp, look at God."

"What do you mean?" It was Belle's turn to give Aria a side-eye.

"They say sometimes He works in ugly ways," Aria answered, leaning back into her seat and getting comfortable. "Maybe us crossing paths wasn't just by chance. Can you play some slow R&B on your phone? We have about a little over an hour until we reach where we need to be. I need to catch a quick nap before I have to shake all this ass."

"Wait. You have a party tonight?"

"Yeah, girl! I just said we have clients in Indy," Aria said. "You don't have to start tonight though, after all that shit. You can just stay on the bus until we're done. Catch a nap or something. I wouldn't even suggest for you to deal with any of these thirsty, greasy motherfuckers tonight." Belle raised her eyebrow, and Aria giggled. "What is it now?"

"You just sound like you . . . care. About me, I mean."

"I don't know you, but when I look into your eyes, I see a lost girl," Aria said, leaning her head on the cold window. "You remind me of myself a few years ago before I met Gene. I was on the streets and alone, broke and hungry."

"And he made you strip for him?"

"He didn't make me do anything. He laid an offer on the table, so I picked it up. Just like the offer I'm laying on the table for you. Nobody is going to put a gun to your head and force you to do anything you don't want to do. However, I have this annoying habit of being so empathetic to the point that it is a weakness. Stranger or not, if you decide to leave when we get to Indy, I'm going to wonder about you for a long time. I'm going to wonder how you're doing and if you're even still alive. So to avoid potential anxiety attacks, I'd rather you be in my face until you get your broke ass back on your feet."

Her voice trailed off, and soon after, a small snore escaped her lips. Aria would never know how much Belle needed to hear those words. She also would never see the small smile that spread over Belle's lips. It was barely noticeable in the stony expression on her face, but it was a smile nonetheless.

Chapter 2

Make the money, don't let it make you.
—The Players Club

"Okay, bitches! You know the drill! Ass out, titties up! Unless a minimum of five hundred is spent, the 'No Touching' rule will be enforced!"

Aria's voice rang out on the luxurious tour bus, and all the young women's attention was on her. She stood at the front of the bus, and the women were in a huddle before her. They didn't break eye contact, and when she was done speaking, they nodded their understanding. Belle sat on the brown leather sectional to the left of them, and it was easy for her to see that Aria was the one in charge there.

They'd finally reached their destination, a hotel in Indianapolis called Hesler's, and when they parked, Aria told her to come inside the tour bus and meet all of the dancers. There were seven other girls, and they were all different shapes and sizes. Five of them were black, one of them was Latina, and one of them was white. They were all pretty and thick in the right places. The tour bus was huge, complete with a master bedroom in the back of it, which the women had used as a dressing room. Belle knew that because the double doors to the huge room were wide open and clothes were strewn everywhere. The outfits the girls now wore gave the strippers Belle had seen on Instagram a run for their money.

"This is Belle," Aria introduced her, and Belle raised her hand in a small wave. "She's going to be joining us."

"She workin' tonight?" a girl in the front of the huddle said. She had caramel skin and long black bundles on top of her head. The deep drawl in her speech made her Southern roots obvious, as did the round bottom behind her.

"No, Luscious, she's going to start tomorrow night. She's going to be the greeter."

"Greeter? You mean she ain't gon' be dancin'?" Luscious asked, making a face.

"Is that a problem?" Aria cut her eyes, and Luscious quickly shook her head.

"Not at all, Lady Passion. I was just gon' say there is more money in dancin', so I don't know why she would wanna be a greeter, that's all."

"Did I force you to dance when you first started with us?"

"No," Luscious said. "But with all this ass behind me, you never had to."

She bent over, placed her hands on her knees, and began twerking. The other girls began to laugh, and even Aria cracked a smile. She looked back at Belle and shook her head.

"These bitches are crazy, but you'll learn that soon enough," she said with a grin and turned back to the women. "Okay, grab your trench coats and get ready to go in. Kidd and the others already went in there and made sure everything was everything and that these white boys aren't on any funny time. Let's go!"

The girls did as they were told and put their matching tan trench coats on, cloaking the fact that they barely had any clothes on. Aria let all of them exit before she looked back at Belle.

"You gon' be all right out here?"

"Yeah," Belle told her and pointed at one of the side bunks. "Is that where I can get some sleep?"

"There?" Aria said and turned her nose up. "Girl, hell no. That's where the niggas sleep. We girls share the room. Enjoy it while the bed is all yours. I'll have Kidd come back out and watch over you until we're done. We shouldn't be longer than four hours. Cool?"

"Cool."

With that, Aria, who had changed into a sexy black teddy with bells on the nipples of it and a tall black pair of stilettos, put on her own trench coat. She winked at Belle before she too was gone. Belle sat there for a few moments and tried not to let her paranoia get the best of her. Not even three hours before, two men had her pinned down in a bathroom, and now she was on a stripper tour bus.

"This is crazy," she said out loud to herself. But as crazy as it was, she couldn't deny that she was beyond tired. Sleep in a comfortable bed sounded like heaven, and when her legs led her to it, she was asleep before her head even hit the pillow.

Her eyes suddenly shot open when she heard somebody moving around the room. She sat up quickly and scooted to the headboard when she saw a man standing at the foot of the bed. He must have recognized the fear on her face, because he held his hands up to show her that he came in peace.

"Who are you?" she asked, and he made a confused face.

"I'm Kidd," he answered in a sexy, deep voice. "You know, from back at the gas station? Aria said she told you I'd be coming back to check on you."

Belle blinked her eyes to make them focus, and when they did, she could honestly say that she did recognize him. Still, that didn't mean she was happy about him interrupting her sleep. She rolled her eyes and crossed her legs Indian style.

"She told me that you would check on me, yes. However, she left out the part where you watch me in my sleep like a creep."

"My bad," he said and rubbed his hand over the dark waves on top of his head. "I guess I would feel some type of way if I woke up and saw a big dude standing over me too."

Belle couldn't help smiling at his joke. But she instantly pursed her lips and tried to glare at him, which made him smile.

"I figured you'd be a mean one, but damn. A brotha can't even get a smile?"

"No, not until you show me that you're not a creep."

"Well, if it means anything, I was sitting in the front of the bus, minding my own business, until you started shouting in your sleep. I came back to check on you, and you were shouting for somebody named Luca? He must be a special guy if he made his way into your dreams."

"He was," Belle said softly. She broke eye contact and stared at her nails. She noticed that the paint had gotten chipped. She tried to focus on that instead of on the innocent face of her baby brother. But it was no use. She could see him smiling with his snaggle teeth clear as day. He had been such a handsome kid with their mom's eyes and their dad's entire face. He had so much life ahead of him. Whoever had taken that away from him deserved to rot in hell for eternity.

"Luca is my little brother," Belle told him. "He died a week ago. Killed in his sleep along with my mom and dad."

"Damn," Kidd said and sat at the foot of the bed, shaking his head. "Damn, shorty, my bad. I didn't know all that."

"Of course you didn't. How could you?"

"Do they know who did it?"

"No. I wasn't even there when it happened. I was away at college. I left after the funeral. I just couldn't stay there. I had to leave and get as far away from that place as I could."

"What about school?" Kidd asked with a serious look on his face. "You just going to drop out?"

"Fuck school," Belle answered. "Plus how am I going to afford tuition if my dad is dead? I left that in the past too."

"You're just going to throw your life away like that?"

"You don't even know me to be trying to give me any type of advice," Belle said, sending a mean glare his way. "I'm going to do whatever it is I have to survive right now."

"Those impulsive decisions are what landed you in the bathroom back at that gas station."

"Yeah? Well, those decisions also landed me on this bus with you. If Aria says I can make some money working the door, then that's what I'm going to do until I figure out my next move."

"Yeah, okay," Kidd scoffed and stood back up.

"What is that supposed to mean?"

"Nothing," Kidd said, shaking his head. "Just that I've never seen any girl come into this game and leave without being forced to. This lifestyle is like a drug, except it's more addictive. The deeper you fall down the rabbit hole, the harder it's going to be to try to climb out."

"I haven't fallen down the rabbit hole yet," Belle responded. "I'm just peeking into it right now."

"All I'm saying is someone as beautiful as you should be in a nice dress suit, not standing at a door with little to no clothes on."

"I'm about to try to go back to sleep before all the girls come back," Belle said, ignoring his last comment. "Will you wake me up so that I can get back in my car and follow y'all to the next stop?"

He nodded once and then made his way back to the front of the bus. She heard him plop down in a seat and grumble something under his breath. She didn't care, though. She just wanted to get in at least one more hour of sleep before they were on the road again. She lay down and got comfortable until once again, sleep found her.

She didn't know how long she'd been out for that time, but when she stirred in her sleep, she smelled a sweet perfume scent. She also noticed that she was under the covers when she distinctly remembered going to sleep on top of them. Opening her eyes, she saw that she was no longer alone in the big bed. To either side of her were all of Gene's Girls, even Aria, passed out asleep. Sitting up slowly so that she wouldn't disturb them, Belle listened to the sounds around her. All was quiet except for the hum of the bus's engine, letting her know that they were now on the move. Before she could panic, a voice stopped her.

"Shh, girl, ain't nobody steal your car. Kidd is driving it, and Jessie is back there with him."

Belle's head whipped to the right, and she saw Luscious sitting at the dimly lit vanity, wiping off her makeup. She was still dressed in the raunchy outfit she had worn when she had left the bus, except she now had a robe draped around her shoulders.

"That's not what I was worried about," Belle lied between her teeth.

"Right," Luscious said, sounding like she didn't believe a word Belle had said.

"I told Kidd to wake me up when you guys got back on the bus."

"And he tried. Hell, we all tried. Bitch, you were knocked out like a damn bear. So we just left you alone, and he grabbed your keys."

"I don't let anyone drive my car," Belle said. "My dad bought it for me."

"And we usually don't pick up strays at gas stations, but here you are," Luscious said and rolled her eyes at Belle through the vanity mirror.

"I'm sorry," Belle sighed, realizing how ungrateful she must have sounded. "I appreciate all of this. Really. I just have a lot on my mind."

"Aria told us that somethin' bad happened to your family," Luscious said and set down her makeup wipe so she could turn to face Belle. "I'm sorry about that."

"Thank you," Belle said and leaned her back on the headboard.

"You ain't got nobody?"

"Nope," Belle said and thought about her uncle. What he had done was unforgivable, so mentioning him was irrelevant. He was dead to her too. "They were my only family."

"Well, now you have a new one," Luscious said with a small smile. "We get a little crazy, but it's all love. You should have come in tonight. Those motherfuckers were throwing mad cash. Woulda given you a chance to see how things go. Can you come and unbutton me in the back? I don't see how those bitches fall asleep in their work clothes."

She waved for Belle to come over to her. Belle hesitated at first, but after a few moments, she carefully made her way off the bed so she wouldn't wake the others. Luscious lifted her robe so that Belle would have access to unhook the teddy from behind, which she did without issue.

"Whoo!" Luscious sighed in relief. "I swear havin' big titties is a gift and a curse. They're always happy to be set free because sheeit! A bitch be feelin' like she's suffocating sometimes."

Belle smiled and watched through the mirror as Luscious briefly got up from the vanity bench and went over to a large suitcase in the corner of the room. From it, she pulled a pair of skintight shorts and a Nicki Minaj

T-shirt to put on. Belle couldn't help it. She couldn't force her eyes to look away as Luscious dropped the robe to her feet. Her body was perfect. Not only did she have round, perky tits and the bottom to match, but her waist was tiny, and her stomach was flat as a board. The long hair on her head gently brushed against her butt cheeks as she stepped into the pair of shorts, and her breasts bounced when she put the shirt over her head. She was mesmerizing to look at, and Belle understood why she was in the line of work she was in. When she turned back around, Belle quickly averted her eyes.

"Girl, I know you were lookin' at me. Don't be shy. I don't think you're gay or nothin'," Luscious said and took her seat once again on the bench. She gave Belle a suspicious look. "That is, unless you are. Gay, that is."

"No!" Belle said and shook her head. "I mean, there was this one time in college I kissed a girl at a party, but I was drunk out of my mind."

"Well, nobody's judgin' you here," Luscious told her and leaned into the mirror to make sure all of the makeup was gone from her face. "Hell, a few of these girls will do anything if the price is right."

"I'm sorry for staring. You're just perfect."

"Perfect?" Luscious looked at her with a bewildered expression and chuckled. "Girl, I'm far from perfect. But you? You just might be the most beautiful woman I have ever seen in my life. Look."

She pointed at Belle's reflection in the mirror and urged her to look at herself. Belle did as she was told, and she studied her own image. Belle had never been the type of girl who was so modest about her looks to the point where she downplayed herself. She knew she was pretty, but it was never something that she allowed to sway her from reality. But at that moment it felt like she was looking at herself for the first time. Even with her hair disheveled a bit on the top of her head, her beauty was undeniable. She rubbed a hand down the right cheek on her slender face and felt the bone in her high cheek-bone. Her full, heart-shaped lips seemed to be frozen in a pucker even when they were relaxed. She batted her long eyelashes and gazed into her own amber eyes, wondering who she was. She wondered if she would ever be the same again.

"See?" Luscious said, interrupting her thoughts. "You see it, don't you?"

"Yes," Belle whispered.

"Door girl my ass. You have potential, baby. What's a little band when you can make five times that?" Luscious said. "It wasn't a coincidence that Lady Passion found you in that bathroom, so a word of advice from one lost soul to the next? Forget who you used to be. I can see you searching for that girl in your eyes right now. She's gone, and she may never come back. Your situation is fresh, but I'm lettin' you know now that if you keep searchin' for that girl, all you will find is pain every time. The only way to heal is to keep going. Keep going and make a hell of a lot of money along the way."

"But how can I forget when I see them every time I close my eyes? My dad. My mom. And my little brother. I still feel it in my chest, you know? It's like someone keeps ripping my heart out and putting it back just to rip it out again."

"You just have to take it day by day, keep yourself busy, keep good company, and stay the hell away from racist gas stations!"

"What would you say about a girl getting on a tour bus full of exotic dancers and contemplating working with them after not even knowing them for a full day?"

"To that, I would say she's either crazy as hell or braver than anybody I've ever met in my life."

Luscious gave a wink and flicked off the light to the vanity before she grabbed Belle's hand to take her back to the bed. Belle climbed over Aria and resumed her spot while Luscious made space toward the bottom. It was like they were cousins all piled up at their grandmother's house. Although it was a tight fit, Belle was strangely comfortable. Her last thought before she fell back to sleep was that she hoped Kidd was driving her car like he had some sense.

Chapter 3

A leader is admired, a boss is feared.
—Vicente del Bosque

"Anthony, what have I told you about touching the merchandise?"

Gene Hightower spoke with a cold tone, and the expression on his face was just as icy. His Dominican features fought against his black ones only to come out equally beautiful. Those very features gave his 58-year-old face a youth that would make one assume he was twenty years younger. His smooth, almond-colored skin always had a radiance to it, giving his handsome face even more allure. There was a flicker of annoyance in his light brown eyes, and three lines appeared on his forehead when he furrowed his brow. His bow-shaped lips were in a straight line as he thought about how he'd come home to relax, not punish.

He had just flown back into Miami after handling some business out of town, and the first place he stopped was the Bliss Lounge. The gentlemen's club that he had built from the ground up was different from any other of its kind. It was much more than a strip club. It was a place of genuine business. Not only that, but in order to even think about walking up to the lounge's door, one must have one of three member-status key cards. The memberships went from Silver to Gold to Black. Each membership came with its own bells and whistles, Silver being entry level and Black being the highest status reserved for the most elite members. Each month, members had to pay a monthly due, which they gladly obliged. Most frequented the club a few times a month, while some came every week, even members who didn't stay in the state. It was a place where one's wildest dreams could come true, and no secret would leave the walls. Gene's motto was, "What is the point of doing business if it isn't a pleasurable experience?"

It had come to Gene's attention that in his absence, one of his workers had taken it upon himself to dabble in the club's amenities. This was something that everyone who worked for him knew was strictly against policy. It was true that the Bliss Lounge had some of the most beautiful women in the nation, and that was why Gene had made sure to hire men who were not easily swayed by the allure of pussy. Or so he thought.

Before him sat a man he'd employed for the past year. Anthony was a dark-skinned brother, mid-30s, and muscular. He'd been hired as an extra security detail for the club, and up until then, he'd done a good job. That was why Gene had made the executive decision to let him off with a warning. They were alone in his office with two of Gene's other workers, who were standing on either side of the door. Anthony sat across from Gene at his mahogany desk, trying to keep a blank expression on his face. But Gene saw past the facade. He could read the fear in Anthony's eyes clear as day.

"What were the conditions upon which you were hired, Anthony?" Gene asked with a straight face.

"To protect your merchandise at all costs, sir," replied Anthony.

"And what exactly is that merchandise?"

"This building, your money, the girls, and the drugs."

"Exactly," Gene said and held a finger up. "Now can you tell me the next clause in our agreement?"

"To not . . ." Anthony paused and cleared his throat. "To not dabble in the amenities, sir, especially when you are on the clock."

"And do you care to explain to me what you have been doing? And before you even think to lie to me, you should know that just because the room isn't finished, that doesn't mean surveillance wasn't already installed."

Anthony didn't answer. Instead, he turned his head and looked at the two men standing by the door. They paid him no mind. Their eyes were looking directly ahead at the wall behind Gene. Anthony swallowed and turned his attention back to his boss, but still, no words came from his mouth.

"What? Cat got your tongue?" Gene said with a chuckle. "No matter, I can recall your recent transgressions. You been digging your dick into Flare, our favorite redheaded gem, every chance you can get. Flare, who may I add, is an exclusive Black Card girl. Not only that, but I have witnessed with my own two eyes the both of you snorting the highest grade of cocaine Miami has to offer. My cocaine . . . which is also only available to Black Card members. Now riddle me this, my dear boy: do you have a Black Card? Because to my knowledge you aren't even a member of the Bliss Lounge."

"It won't ever happen again, sir," Anthony said and clasped his hands together. "She just kept coming on to me and . . . and . . . you've seen her!"

"And what do you think I should do about your disobedience?"

"I . . . it won't ever happen again. I promise, sir. If you let me walk out of this room, I won't even look Flare's way again. Please."

The way his voice shook as he spoke was proof that Gene's reputation preceded him. If Anthony only knew that the things in the wind about Gene were the PG version of the truth, he would have soiled his pants. No, he would have never even looked Flare's way, because he would know the nightmare sure to follow. Gene's lips spread to a small smile, and he nodded slightly.

"I guess it works out for you that I'm in good spirits," Gene said. "I'm willing to let you go with a warning."

"Thank you, sir," Anthony said and shook his clasped hands. "Thank you."

"No thanks needed," Gene said and opened one of the drawers to his desk. "Forgiveness is something I learned on a trip that I made to Japan a few years back. I learned to forgive, but only at the sincerest form of apology."

From the drawer, he pulled out a small wooden board, and on it was a small knife. He tested the blade and, when he was satisfied with its sharpness, slid it and the board over to Anthony. Clasping his own hands, he took pleasure in the bewildered expression on Anthony's face.

"*Yubitsume,*" Gene said simply. "A ritual to atone for your wrongdoings here, Anthony, and all will be forgiven. Your pinky will do just fine."

"You want me to cut off my own finger?"

"Not all of it, just the part right above your knuckle there," Gene said and pointed to it. "I am willing to let you walk out of here with your life and your job. But even warnings come with a punishment."

Anthony knew that the man sitting before him was serious. He looked from Gene back to the men guarding the door and saw that there was no way out. He swallowed a big gulp of air because all the liquid in his mouth had dried up, and with a shaky hand, he picked up the knife. Placing his left hand with the palm down on the board, he positioned the knife over his pinky finger. The blade on the knife was so sharp that it instantly sliced his skin. Seeing the blood trickle slowly down his finger brought him to what he thought were his senses. He stopped abruptly and dropped the knife back on the board.

"No," he said defiantly, pushing the board back to Gene. "This ain't no old fucking Japanese movie. I'll pay whatever debt you believe I owe you, but I'm not cutting off my own finger."

Gene glanced down at the board that was now back in front of him. His eyes lingered on the few drops of Anthony's blood as they seeped into the wood, leaving only a dark red stain behind. He felt nothing and everything at the same time at Anthony's contempt.

"I have no use for someone who isn't willing to cut off his finger to save his hand," he said. "Maybe if you knew the price of your debt was your life, that small piece of your finger would be in front of me right now."

He gestured his pointer finger slightly, giving the men behind Anthony a signal. Without further ado, they removed their guns and fired them as soon as they were aimed. The shocked expression was frozen on Anthony's face when the back of his head was blown off, and his brain particles flew every which way.

"Ugh," Gene scoffed and removed the handkerchief from his suit pocket. "I just got this desk. Could you have been less messy?"

"Sorry, boss."

"No matter. This is exactly why I removed the carpet from my office. Cleaning the stains out of it was getting quite expensive. Get him out of here and clean up the mess," Gene said, swiveling in his chair. "And when you're done send Flare to me. I have to give her the bad news. She's fired."

"Yes, sir," one of them said to the back of his chair. Gene didn't know which one, nor did he care. As long as they did as they were told.

His eyes found solace in the painting that was on the wall behind his desk. It was a custom piece he had painted of an above shot of the city of Miami. His city. He didn't run it with an iron fist, nor was he a big drug lord. He ran it with the power of pussy. Gene knew that even the most powerful man in the world fell victim to the charm of women, and he used that to his advantage. The Bliss Lounge was what he called the "main office." However, he had shops just like it set up all over the nation and was still expanding. He even had a traveling tour bus that frequented his first-class customers twice a year. He figured it was a way to pay homage for their loyal business. Why make them come to him when he could send the pleasure to them? Gene's Girls, of course, were accompanied by the sharpest shooters he had to offer to ensure the safety of his commodities. Only his best girls were allowed to travel the tour under the supervision of his head girl, Lady Passion. She wasn't his oldest girl, but she'd proven many times over to be the most loyal. He trusted her.

Bzzz! Bzzz! Bzzz!

The phone vibrating violently in his pocket snatched him from his thoughts. Behind him, he heard his workers still picking up brain particles and dragging Anthony's body from his office. Gene took his cell phone from his pocket and answered immediately when he saw who was calling.

"Aria, is everything all right? It's only one o'clock in the afternoon. This isn't your usual check-in time."

"I know, but I wanted to call and let you know what's going on before we reach Detroit and one of your other employees tells you."

"What happened?" Gene asked, sitting up a little straighter in his seat.

"Nothing bad. It's just . . ." Aria paused as if she were trying to get the balls to spit it out. "It's just I recruited another girl. She's on the bus with us right now."

"You recruited another girl without first consulting with me?"

"Yes. I found her at a gas station in Illinois. These men were trying to rape her, Gene. I couldn't leave her there."

"You've seen worse things than a girl about to be raped, Aria. What made you allow a complete stranger passage onto my tour bus?"

"She . . . she reminds me of myself, Gene. I saw myself when I looked into her eyes. I think it's what you must have seen when you found me."

"What is this girl's name?"

"Belle."

"Belle for beauty. Tell me, what does she look like?"

"Exactly like her name. Ten times beyond it if I'm being completely honest. I told her that she could work as a greeter until we get back to Miami. She doesn't have anybody, Gene. Her entire family is dead. I just couldn't leave her."

"Aria—"

"You wanted to see me, sir?" a sweet voice interrupted him as he was talking.

Gene swiveled his chair back around and saw Flare standing in front of him, wearing nothing but a red sultry dominatrix outfit with tall stilettos. The red hair on her head was pulled up into a long, high ponytail, and even Gene had to admit that she was very tantalizing. Still, that would not give her vindication for what she had done. One of the same employees who had just done Anthony in was standing behind her, and he slowly shut the door to the office.

"Now that I think about it," Gene said into the phone, "a slot just opened up. But we don't need a greeter. If she isn't entertaining, she has to go."

He disconnected the phone before Aria could say another word, and he gave Flare his undivided attention. He observed as her eyes skimmed over his office and saw the traces of blood still there. He smiled at her when those same eyes found his own.

"Flare, tsk tsk," he said. "You've been a very, very bad girl."

Chapter 4

Life is a journey that must be traveled no matter how bad the roads and accommodations.
—Oliver Goldsmith

After spending a couple of days with the girls, Belle didn't even want to drive her own car, and she was sure that Kidd didn't mind it much. He was having a ball pushing her hemi engine to the edge, and she was having a ball getting to know the girls. Besides Aria and Luscious, there were Cream, Russian Roulette, Dynasty, Blessing, and Drip. Russian Roulette may have been the only white girl, but she definitely had the soul of a sister. Belle could tell Cream had a little temper on her. Whenever she got irritated, she would go off on a Spanish rant, and nobody could understand what she was saying. Dynasty kept to herself mostly, but that mainly had to do with the fact that the weed she smoked kept her pretty mellow. Blessing and Drip were sisters and were almost spitting images of each other. If you didn't know they were two years apart, you would think they were twins.

Two days had passed since Aria had found Belle and since her conversation with Luscious. It was strange how two days could feel like an eternity. They had finally made it to Detroit, and the first thing on all of their minds was the mall.

"I need some new shoes!" Russian Roulette said as she sat on the floor, wearing nothing but a T-shirt. She had been going through her suitcase and turning her nose up at all of her items. "And, Drip, I ain't letting you borrow no more of my shit! You never give it back. I have to buy new everything."

"Girl, hush," Drip said from where she was halfway off of the bed. Her long hair was folded on the ground, and she had her phone up in the air as she was scrolling through her social media feeds. "Can't nobody take that little squeaky voice of yours serious."

"I don't know why you would want that shit back anyways. Her pussy juices done soiled the material by now," Luscious commented from her favorite spot, the vanity.

"I can't help it if money makes me cum," Drip said and sat upright, running her hands through her hair. She rolled her eyes in Luscious's direction. "You're always jumping into something with your country ass."

"I'd rather be from the country than from Wyoming," Luscious threw back. "I didn't even know there were black people there. You might as well be from Maine like Russian Roulette."

"You know what? Just finish your makeup before I throw some pussy-juice panties at your face," Drip said. They all laughed, including Belle.

"Y'all are too loud!" Dynasty's groggy voice sounded from the bed and underneath the covers. "Some people are still trying to sleep."

"Bitch, if you don't get your high ass up . . . It's one o'clock!" Luscious dropped the makeup brush from her hands and got up. She went over to the bed and snatched the cover back. "You, Blessing, and Cream need to wake up."

"No," Cream whined and tried to grab the comforter. "Five more minutes! Please!"

"How about no more minutes? I told your ass about drinking all that tequila last night."

"It was my off day!" Cream whined again.

"Bitch, it was all of our off days!" Russian Roulette giggled. "You didn't see any of us getting white girl wasted, no pun intended."

"That's because you are all some prude bitches," Cream said and reluctantly sat up. Her shoulder-length hair was disheveled all over her head, and she rocked the puffy-lipped "just woke up" look as she glared around the room.

"I can't believe you just called a bus full of strippers prudes," Drip laughed and nudged Cream playfully with her toe. "She must still be drunk."

"No, I'm not. I'm . . ." Cream paused and grabbed Drip's whole foot in her hands. "Girl, is this my new Pink Volt nail polish?"

"No!" Drip said and snatched her foot back.

The guilty expression on her face let Belle know that she was lying. Cream knew it too, because the next words out of her mouth were all Spanish. Russian Roulette rolled her eyes and went back to sorting through her suitcase while Belle went back to observing her. The only things she kept were her jeans and dressy blouses. Everything else she put to the side.

"Are you throwing that stuff away?" Belle asked, and Russian Roulette looked at her like she was crazy.

"Girl, hell no. We usually hit a laundromat every three days while we're on the road. I honestly should have washed them at the hotel we stayed in last night. Some of these pieces cost a pretty penny, and one thing we don't do here is throw away money."

"Oh," was all Belle said.

"You must have been one of them rich girls, huh? You come from a family with money, don't you?"

"What?"

"I'm just saying. Most college girls can't afford a 2018 Camaro, let alone be laced in designer clothes."

"Oh. Yeah. My dad owned a large company. I don't really know much about what he did. I just know he helped his clients invest large amounts of money into things that would make them even more money. And that made him money. Lots of it."

"So how did you end up with only five hundred dollars to your name?"

"Russian!" Luscious's voice sounded.

Belle looked up to see that the five other girls had eased their way to the edge of the bed and were giving her and Russian Roulette's conversation their full attention.

"What? I'm just asking."

"It's okay," Belle assured Luscious with a small smile and turned back to Russian Roulette. "My dad isn't . . . wasn't really my birth dad. He married my mom when I was five. He was killed before he added me or my mother to his will. I know it's something he should have done a long time ago, but I'm sure he thought he had plenty of time to do so. All of his stuff, including the business, went to his older brother, my uncle."

"And he didn't give you a dime?"

"No," Belle told them. "And I didn't plan on sticking around to beg him for my father's money."

"He hasn't called you since you've been gone?"

"Not once. But that doesn't surprise me. He never liked me. Or my mother."

"He told you?"

"No. You know how there are just some things you can feel? Whenever he was around, I just felt like he was annoyed by my presence."

"Yo, this sounds like one of those Lifetime movies," Cream said, and everyone except Belle glared at her. "What? No, I'm serious. He probably killed his brother so he could take over and get everything."

"He wasn't in town when it happened," Belle told her. "My uncle is a selfish man, but he isn't a killer."

"He could have hired someone to do it," Drip suggested. "You know people with long money can do that."

"Well, his money isn't long. I mean, it is now," Belle said, shaking her head. Suddenly she was getting the onset of a headache. "I just don't think he did it. Like I said, he's selfish and mean, but he's kind of dumb. He worked for my dad's company, but I'm sure he has no idea what he's doing now. I give him a year before he's flat broke. My dad always said he would lose his own hands if they weren't attached to his body."

"Well, you're with us now, sugar," Russian Roulette said. "Blood couldn't make us any closer."

"But money can!" Drip shouted as Aria made her entrance in the room.

She had her phone in her hand and an unreadable look on her face. She was the only one out of them all who was fully dressed. She wore a burgundy tunic sweater that hugged her body and stopped at her thighs, a pair of light brown leggings, and a pair of Fendi combat boots. She still rocked her ninja bun, and her makeup looked beat by the gods. Her eyes trailed over all of them, and she made a face.

"I'm guessing none of you hoes wants to go shopping? We're about to be at the mall. Get dressed!" On her command, everyone but Belle started moving.

"All my clothes are in the trunk of my car." Belle stood up and motioned to the shorts and T-shirt she had on. "I only grabbed this when we stopped at the hotel last night to throw on after I showered. If we pull over real quick, I can go grab something."

"Girl, stop," Luscious said and sized her up. "I think you can fit in my clothes. You're thick enough. I think I even have some panties in here I've never worn before."

Luscious dug into her suitcase and pulled out a lowcut black body suit, a pair of light-washed distressed jeans, a thong with the tag still attached, and a pair of socks.

"Here, boo," she said and handed over the clothing. "Now, baby, I don't know what size shoe you wear, but I'm a size six, and most people's feet are bigger than that."

"Yeah, I'm a size seven," Belle said, taking the clothes.

"Me too. I have some cute Gucci boots you can wear," Aria said, stepping over Russian Roulette's bag to get to her own suitcases. She pulled the boots out. "Here. And wait, put these on, too. And oh! Wait. Carry this, too."

She handed Belle two gold chains to put around her neck and a Gucci crossbody bag to match the boots. Belle hesitated before she took them. "Thank you."

"Don't mention it. We go everywhere looking like we have bands in our bags, because we do," Aria said and winked. "Now hurry up and get dressed. I know you took a shower at the hotel, but you know where the bathroom is. The shower isn't operational, but the sinks work if you want to freshen up."

"Don't be ashamed, girl! If a bitch claim she ain't never took a ho bath, she's lying!"

Belle laughed at Drip's outburst as she took her clothes to the bathroom to get ready. When she was done, she looked in the mirror, and for the first time since receiving that dreadful phone call, she looked like herself again. Not the old her, but the new her. The one with sadness still in her eyes but the will to welcome new life and smile. She'd braided her hair into two French braids and pinned them in the back. She was happy that one of the others had left some gel and a hair toothbrush in the bathroom so she could do her edges. She put on a coat of lip gloss and gave herself one last look.

"We're here! Come on, Belle! I'm tryin' to go into Saks and clean that bitch out!" Luscious yelled and banged on the bathroom door. "Y'all bitches tryin'a leave me?" she yelled at the other girls before she banged on the door again. "Come on, girl!"

Belle opened the bathroom door and looked down the long hallway on the bus to see the girls filing off. She grabbed her coat so she could hurry after them, and when she got off, she ran right into Kidd.

"Mmm," she said and looked him up and down.

He smiled from ear to ear and licked his lips sexily at her. "Damn! I can't even stand here doing nothing without you giving me attitude," Kidd said to her.

"Whatever," Belle said with a grin. "I just know you better be driving my damn car right."

"Trust me, I am," he said and then eyed her mischievously. "With you looking like that, I might just have to drive you next."

"You better stop," she said and playfully hit his arm.

"You right," Kidd said. He then motioned to the other girls and security who were halfway to the Neiman Marcus entrance at the Somerset Collection mall. "We better catch up before they buy up this place. The last time we went to the mall, they collectively spent fifty bands in that bitch. Wait, you got some bread?"

Suddenly it dawned on Belle that all she had left was $200. The only place she would be able to shop with that was Forever 21. Kidd read the sheepish expression on her face, reached into his own pocket, and pulled out a roll of hundreds.

"I'm sure Aria is gon' hook you up, but here's a start," Kidd said and put it in her hand but didn't let go. "This is five bands, and I'ma only give it to you if you spend it all in here."

"All of it? But then I'm going to be broke again."

"You with us, shorty. You ain't never broke. If we got it, you got it. Period."

There was something about the way the words rolled off of his tongue that gave Belle butterflies. She didn't know if it was because Kidd was sexy and boss as hell, even though he was so young, or if it was because she knew he meant it. He let the money go when she nodded, and the two of them followed everyone else.

"So, Belle, what is it that you wanna do with your life?" Kidd asked as they were walking.

"Do you really care?"

"I wouldn't ask if I didn't."

"I guess the honest answer to that question is I don't know now," she said and shrugged. "I was in school to become a veterinarian, but even though that was a little over a week ago, it seems so far away. You know? Losing my parents like that has really made me rethink so much shit, and now it's like, did I really want to be that? Or did I want to just do something fun because my dad was rich and I wouldn't have to worry about money?"

"Being a vet sounded fun to you?"

"Oh, yeah." Belle nodded. "I love animals. Their lives are so simple."

"So what's the move now?"

"I sent an email the day of my family's funeral telling the school I wouldn't be back. Going to school right now would just be too hard. I wouldn't be able to focus. And I wouldn't be able to bear all of those sorry expressions and the sympathy. It would have driven me mad."

"I get that, but you didn't answer my question."

"What question?"

"What's the move now?" Kidd asked again.

By then, they had reached the entrance doors to Neiman Marcus, and he held one of them open for her to go through first. They walked in the store, and as she looked around, she also thought about his question.

"I guess work and save enough money to move some-where."

"And where might that be?" he asked, and a big smile spread across her lips.

"Don't laugh at me," she said, rolling her eyes and shaking her head.

"Me? Laugh at you? Never!"

"See! I'm not telling you nothing!"

"Nah, for real though. Let me know. Where you wanna go, shorty? I might've been there before."

"California."

"Why would I laugh at that? Cali is the place to be, for real though. I done been in and out that place plenty of times."

"Because it's so cliché, you know? Who doesn't want to live in Cali? I just have always loved huge bodies of water and warm weather. And it's so beautiful there, even though they have really bad storms. But hell, I lived in Nebraska where we got blizzards, so I guess it would just be a trade." She shrugged and touched a designer bag as they walked by it. "California is so expensive, though. I'm probably going to have to be a door girl for a while before I can make that move."

"As long as you stack up and don't lose focus on your goal, you can do it," Kidd told her and linked his arm in hers.

"Says the guy who's telling me to blow five thousand dollars in the mall."

"Hey wait, don't be using my words against me now!" he said and leaned his warm body into hers. "You're living out of a trunk, man. You probably only got like eight outfits in there. You're too bad to be living like that."

"That's the second time you complimented me," Belle said and gave him a playful smirk. "Either you like me or you feel sorry for me. Which one is it?"

"Maybe a little of both," he said as they walked.

"Well, I don't want you to feel sorry for me. I don't want anyone to feel sorry for me."

"Listen, anyone who has felt loss is gon' feel sorry for you. So don't take it as pity, especially coming from me. I respect that you didn't give in to that pain, because most people do. They can't see the other side of the tunnel."

"And what's on the other end of the tunnel?"

"You," he said simply. "The person you're going to be when you allow yourself to be happy again."

His words took her breath away. She didn't know how someone so young could be so insightful. She would expect that kind of wisdom from an old head, not someone her age. Speaking of which, she realized she didn't know much of anything about the man driving her car.

"How old are you, Kidd? And is Kidd even your real name?"

"Girl, you know Kidd ain't my real name. It's just a little nickname I got when I was younger since I was always kidding around. That was before the streets turned me into a savage, though. I'm twenty-five now, and I'm from Miami, Florida, before you ask. Born and raised."

"That's how you got this job then, huh? Working for Gene, I mean."

"Yeah, I did a job for him a while back, and he liked how I moved, so he hired me on a security detail for his main club. After a few years, I earned his respect, and now I look after his best girls. He pays me good to be a babysitter, too. 'Cause them girls be wildin' sometimes."

"Oh, I can already tell," Belle giggled. "But I really appreciate them. All of y'all, to be honest. Not even because of the gas station shit. But because I just don't feel alone anymore. That's the worst feeling. Being alone."

"Trust me, I know," Kidd said, stopping by the women's shoe section. He unhooked his arm from hers. He picked up a pair of black Louboutin stilettos and waved a worker over to help them. "She needs these in a size . . . What's your size, shorty?"

"Seven," Belle answered and put her hand on her hip, cocking her head. "But how do you know I even like those?"

"Because you do," Kidd grinned and turned back to the older woman. "She likes them, and she'll take them. You can just hold them up at the front."

"Oh, so you're the controlling type, I see," she teased.

"Never that. I just think your frame would look good in those shoes. Plus any woman who looks like you deserves a pair of red bottoms. Ten pairs to be real."

"You don't even know how much they cost," Belle said, not being able to lie and say she didn't like them.

"I haven't had to look at a price tag in years now," Kidd said modestly and checked the diamond-studded Rolex on his wrist. "But go 'head and get your shop on. The others are probably looking for you. I'll be around."

She gave him a one-armed hug before she took off in the direction of Luscious's loud Southern drawl. Granted, Belle's father was a very wealthy man, but he never let her just go crazy in the mall. Even when she was in college, she only got a monthly allowance of $1,500. She had a few designer pieces that were gifts, but other than that she'd lived like a pretty regular girl. Shopping with Gene's Girls made her feel like a girl in a candy shop.

Like Kidd said, Aria hooked her up too. As soon as Belle caught up to them, she handed her $3,000 out of her own purse, and they got busy. When they were done in Neiman, they had so much stuff they had to run back outside to unload before they went to any other store. Belle was having so much fun being dragged around by Luscious, and she didn't complain one bit.

"Ooh! Let's go in here, Belle! We need to get you some pieces to wear tonight anyways!" Luscious said and grabbed her new friend by the hand when they walked by a sexy lingerie boutique. "Come on. That black thing right there would be cute on you . . . or me. Shit, we can both get it. Just come on!"

Belle was so busy laughing that she hadn't even noticed that Aria had fallen behind and was walking side by side with Kidd. Aria waited for Belle to be out of earshot and in the boutique before grabbing Kidd by the arm and looking curiously into his eyes.

"You gave her some money?" she asked him, and he shrugged his shoulders.

"Why do you ask?"

"Because I only gave her three thousand and she went over that in Neiman," Aria told him.

"I mean, I gave her a little something something," he answered like it was no big deal, and she let him go.

"I'm not tripping on that," Aria sighed and waved for him to follow her to a bench in the middle of the mall. "Come talk to me."

"What's up?" Kidd asked when they sat down. Instead of answering him, Aria just looked at him. She looked at him for so long that Kidd started grinning. "What, dude?"

"You like her, don't you?"

"What?"

"Yeah, you like her," Aria said. She shook her head and gave him a knowing look. "You know how Gene is about his girls. He doesn't like his workers to dabble with each other."

"Well, technically she ain't one of his girls. She's just a greeter."

"About that . . ." Aria sighed and looked away.

"About what?" Kidd asked.

"I talked to Gene on the way here," she said and watched Belle through the window of the boutique. Belle was holding up an oversized thong and pretending to put it on Luscious's head. Even though Aria and Belle were the same age, her innocence showed in the most simple ways. The smile that spread on Aria's lips was a sad one.

"You told him about Belle?"

"Yeah, I did. And he said he doesn't need any greeters."

"Okay, well, that's even better," Kidd said with a grin.

"Kidd." Aria shook her head. "He wants her to dance. And if I tell her that, she's going to want to dance."

"How do you know that?"

"Because even though you can't see it, I can. She's already attached."

"Attached to what, Aria? She ain't even done shit yet."

"By just being around us, she's done everything. She's gotten a taste of this lifestyle, and given the choice to have this or nothing? What would you choose?"

"So why don't you just tell her that Gene doesn't want her? Tell her that there isn't any openings."

"Because if I do, she'll leave. And she has nothing right now, Kidd. I can't do that to her. Not when I'm the one who gave her a reason to push through in the first place. The girl we met a few days ago and the girl she is now are two different people. You can't see that? I know what it feels like to have nothing and nobody. I'm not saying this is the best life, but it's better than where I would have ended up."

"She might be different."

"Nah," Aria said, wishing it weren't true. "She's not. I don't know what kind of pain you've felt in your life. But losing your people and then being robbed of everything that reminds you of who you are as a person is a different thing. I just keep thinking about what if we hadn't stopped at that gas station. She would probably be dead in a ditch somewhere. Don't nobody care about us. But dancing? Contrary to what people may feel about girls like me, dancing gives you a way to take all that control back. It's a way to learn your self-worth, and everyone around you just worships the ground you walk on. That's the kind of power she needs right now. And after she learns her place in the world again, I'll let her go."

"You say that like she's your property."

"No, but I'm very drawn to her. And until I know why, she is my responsibility."

"So you throw her into Gene's world?" Kidd asked incredulously. "You know just like I know what he's capable of."

"I know."

"So what then?"

"I'm going to tell her that Gene wants her to dance," Aria said and then looked him square in the eyes. "And I'm telling you now to leave her alone. As you said, you and I both know what Gene is capable of. You are her security, that's it. If it becomes a problem, I'll send you back to Miami. I love you like a brother, Kidd, and I don't want temptation to be a reason why something happens to you. It's just business, Kidd. I'm sorry."

With that, she got up to head into the lingerie store, leaving Kidd to stare at Belle's smiling face, feeling a longing that he'd never be able to satisfy.

Chapter 5

The body of a beautiful woman is not
made for love; it is too exquisite.
        —Henri de Toulouse-Lautrec

After they left the mall, they stopped at a family-owned restaurant called Clippers. That time Belle was the first off the bus, and when she saw Kidd parking her car, she waved and proceeded to wait for him. He smiled at her as he got out of the car and started walking her way.

"Girl, you're acting like you aren't hungry," Aria said and linked arms with her so they could walk in together.

"I was just waiting for Kidd," Belle answered and looked back only to see that Cream was walking next to him.

"Let that man do his job. All I want to do is get a nice, juicy burger and some fries so that I can stuff my face!"

Belle gave Kidd one last look, but he was too busy smiling in Cream's face to notice. Instead of dwelling too much on him, Belle decided to enjoy the rest of the time she had before her first night of work. She wondered how greeting people would go and if they would try to touch her. She was almost certain that the job would require her to be bubbly and flirty, which wouldn't be a problem. She considered herself to be a professional at getting guys to buy her drinks at the bar, so getting men ready to spend money on strippers shouldn't be too hard.

"How many today?" the petite hostess asked when they were all inside the doors.

"Eleven," Aria answered.

"All right. One second while we get you a table ready."

She left, and while she was gone, Belle took in the restaurant. It was set up pretty much like any other restaurants with booths, tables, a bar, and some big-screen TVs. Still, the warm aroma coming from the kitchen mixed with the old-school tunes gave her an "at home" vibe. The hostess returned in a matter of minutes to grab their menus and motion for them all to follow her. She seated them toward the back of the restaurant by a beautiful mural of a black woman reading a book. Her natural curls were everything, and her beauty dripped from the photo.

"Your server, Jack, will be right with you," she said, and with a smile, she was gone.

"If his last name isn't Daniels, I don't want him," Russian Roulette joked.

"I'm sure you'll get plenty of that tonight," Blessing said.

"Uh-uh," Aria told them. "No dark liquor for any of you. Y'all don't know how to act when y'all drink that shit. Tonight we will be servicing some of Gene's best clients. I need you all to be on your best behavior."

"We will if they are," Luscious said with a sly smile.

"They better be, unless they want this steel up their ass," Jay, a member of their security team, said and patted his hip.

"On me, if they get to acting, we gon' get it cracking!" Kevo, who was sitting next to him, said. They slapped hands.

Belle hadn't really gotten to know them. The only time she'd ever seen them speak was to each other and to Aria. They were big, and she could tell by looking in their eyes that they had seen some things that didn't need to be repeated in their lives. Although they had youthful features, Belle couldn't pinpoint their age, and she wouldn't ask either. Kidd had been the only one who had made himself personable, or even approachable for that matter.

"That's why Gene always sends y'all with us, because you keep us so safe," Russian Roulette flirted, but neither Jay or Kevo batted an eye.

It was as if they hadn't even heard her, and Belle saw Aria shoot her a look that she couldn't read. The rest of them opened their menus and began glancing through, trying to figure out what they wanted. Belle didn't need to look at the menu to know what she wanted. What Aria said on the way inside the restaurant sounded delicious, except Belle wanted bacon on her burger.

"How are we doing this afternoon, folks?" a chipper voice came out of nowhere, making them all look up.

The voice belonged to a lanky Caucasian young man with glasses on his face. He had thick red hair on top of his head, which matched his cherry-colored lips. The black shirt he wore said the word "Clippers" above his right breast bone, and his jeans were so blue they had to have been brand new. He seemed so happy that you couldn't help but be happy with him.

"You must be Jack," Aria said with a smile.

"That would be me."

"Well, we're all doing fine," she said and turned to everyone at the table. "Are y'all ready to order? Because I am, and I'm not waiting if you want to be indecisive."

"I am," Belle spoke up, and Jack looked her way.

It wouldn't have been weird if he had said something, but he didn't. Instead, he just stared, almost as if he were in a trance. He didn't even budge when Aria waved her hand in his face. It wasn't until she poked him that he snapped out of it.

"Oh, my," he said, shaking his head and looking at Belle again. His face had gone completely red. "I'm sorry. I just . . . I guess I've never seen anyone as beautiful as you in my entire life. All of you actually."

"Well, thank you," Aria said, and gave Belle a smirk. "Go ahead and tell him what you want to order, Belle."

"Oh, wow, your name means beauty, too," Jack said and pulled out a small notebook. "So fitting. What would you like to eat, Beauty? I mean, Belle."

"Uhhh," Belle said and looked around the table wide-eyed before she cleared her throat. "Can I just have your best bacon cheeseburger with lettuce and tomato with some fries and a side of ranch?"

"Definitely. What for your drink?" Jack asked.

"A water is just fine, thank you," Belle told him, and he jotted it down.

"And for you?" Jack said, continuing to go around the table.

When he'd gotten everybody's orders, he looked at Belle one last time and disappeared to the kitchen.

"Okay, Belle has the juice!" Blessing teased.

"Stop it." She rolled her eyes, but even she couldn't pretend like she wasn't flattered.

Jack brought their drinks back to the table, and that time, he didn't get all tripped up at the sight of Belle. After that, they all made small talk as they were waiting for their food to come from the kitchen. Belle kept noticing Aria giving her weird looks, but that wasn't stranger than Kidd acting as if she didn't exist. He was talking to everyone else but hadn't looked her way. She didn't understand.

It took about twenty minutes for them to get their food and about half of that time for them to scarf it down. When they were done, the guys handled the bill and left Jack a hefty tip. After stuffing themselves full of wings, burgers, and fries, the girls headed back to the tour bus to prepare for the night. They were staying in a hotel suite so that everyone could rest up for the long trip to Memphis. Before Belle could climb back on, Aria grabbed her by the arm and pulled her aside to talk to her.

"Hey, how are you feeling about tonight?" she asked.

"A little nervous," Belle responded, "but I'll be all right. All I have to do is smile and direct people where to go, right?"

"About that," Aria said and clenched her eyes shut for a moment. "Belle, I'm sorry. I talked to Gene earlier today, and he said he doesn't need a greeter."

Belle's face dropped, and when Aria opened her eyes, all she saw was the disappointment written all over it.

"Okay, so what? Are you telling me that I have to leave now?"

"No! That's not what I'm saying at all. I'm saying that he said he doesn't need a greeter. He said he wants you to dance."

"Dance?"

"Yes. Like what we do," Aria told her. "I tried to tell him—"

"Okay."

"Huh?"

"Okay. I'll dance." Belle shrugged like it wasn't a big deal.

"Just okay? That's all you have to say?"

"Yeah. I kind of figured I would have to dance eventually. I mean, if someone ever asked me before what I pictured doing with my life, stripping would be the furthest thing from my mind. But I also wouldn't have said I'd be an orphan either, so fuck it. It is what it is."

"Are you sure?"

"What other option do I have, Aria? I mean, seriously. Go work at some bar or a mall somewhere? So yes, I'm positive. I blew eight thousand dollars today on clothes and shoes. I don't know the last time I felt so free."

"There's a lot more where that came from," Aria told her. "I'm so glad you aren't mad at me."

"Mad at you? No."

"Well, if you want, you can sit tonight out and just watch us work."

"I'll work. I don't know much about working a pole, but I know how to dance," Belle said.

"All right." Aria studied Belle for a second before nodding her approval. "It's settled then. Come on so the girls can brief you on all of the rules to this shit."

Twerk
Girl, I wanna see you twerk
I'll throw a li'l money if you twerk

Blac Youngsta's voice snuck its way under the bathroom door where Belle was trying not to psych herself out. Earlier she'd made it seem as if dancing was going to be a breeze, but saying was much easier than doing. Although the girls had told her what to do and what to expect, she still was beyond nervous. Once they reached the mansion in Southfield and got to the door, they entered single file with Aria, aka Lady Passion, at the front of the line so she could introduce the ladies behind her. It didn't dawn on Belle that she hadn't even selected a name for herself until she was the only one left outside of the door, wearing nothing but a trench coat over the hot pink bra and thong set she had on. However, Aria had that part covered too.

"Last but not least," she'd said in a commanding voice, "I have a treat for you boys tonight. We have a newww giiirrrllll!" The people inside went wild with excitement. "Settle down before you make her too timid to come in and party with you guys. I want y'all to treat her nice, okay? Now tell me something, sugars, what have you heard about Nebraska girls? Welcome . . . Beauty!"

Belle's legs had felt like Jell-O as she forced them to move and tried to ignore the cold nipping at her body. Once she was inside the foyer, she was met with ten sets of eyes staring lustfully at her. The men were standing in front of the spiral staircase, and the other girls were standing to the side with sexy smirks frozen on their faces. When the set of double doors closed behind her, Belle did as she was coached to do earlier. She smiled at the gentlemen before her, struck the sexiest pose that she could, and let the trench coat she was wearing slide to the floor. The moment her curves were revealed in her pink thong, she could have sworn time stopped the way it seemed the men stopped breathing. Belle's eyes found Kidd, who was standing with Kevo and Jay behind the other girls. He didn't blink as he stared at her, and his mouth fell open ever so slightly.

"Damn, I need alone time with her!" one of the men said, finally breaking the silence.

"We always save the best for last," Aria said. "Now let the festivities begin! We need music, and where are the motherfucking bottles?"

Everything after that began to move so fast, too fast. One minute Belle was standing in the foyer, and the next she was in the basement of the gigantic home with strobe lights and loud music. In the middle of the floor, there was a pole that Drip and Blessing wasted no time going to. Aria, who must have been used to being the center of attention, went right to the center of the basement.

"Now you fellas are all Black Card members at the Bliss Lounge, so I'm already knowing you know the rules right? No touching unless you have individually given the woman you want quality time with five hundred dollars minimum! And I know y'all want to have a good time in this bitch, don't you?"

"Yeah!" they all yelled in unison.

"I don't think I heard you!" Aria yelled. She turned around, bent over to grab her ankles, and dropped down in a split. Her huge bottom shook like an earthquake as she bounced up and down. "I said do you want to have a good time in here tonight?"

"Hell yeah!"

A few of the men whistled while others threw hundred-dollar bills at her. The men were all clean-cut and looked as if they were made of money. They were all shapes, colors, and sizes. The other girls went straight into entertainment mode, and more money began getting thrown instantly. Belle didn't know how they kept track of who threw $500, but the floor was already covered in hundred-dollar bills.

"Can I get a dance, Beauty? I'd like to be your first of the night."

The deep voice came up behind Belle and caught her off guard. When she turned around, she found herself face-to-face with a tall, light-skinned fellow. He was wearing a suit, and his cologne smelled heavenly. He was very handsome, but still, at that moment, Belle started to feel sick to her stomach. The way he looked at her and licked his lips made her feel like a spectacle. Because she was. It was like she was in a circus and she was the star attraction. It was all too much to take in at one time, and she needed to find a bathroom before she threw up all over herself.

"I'll be right back," she said and winked at him before sashaying away, careful not to trip over her six-inch heels.

And that was how she wound up in the basement's bathroom.

"Okay, okay, okay," Belle said to her reflection as she took many deep breaths in and out. "Am I really doing this? I'm really doing this. What the fuck?"

She wanted to throw some cold water over her face, but Luscious had worked so hard on her makeup that night. Why hadn't she just stayed back at the hotel? Or even better, why hadn't she taken Aria up on her offer to just observe that night? Instead, there she was about to completely shit her pants because one guy asked her for a dance.

Knock! Knock!

"Just a second," Belle said when she heard someone outside the door. "I'll be right out!"

"Or you can let me in, little mama," Belle heard Drip's voice say.

Belle hesitated at first, but after a second she unlocked the door and let Drip inside. Drip pushed the door back, but she didn't shut it all the way behind her. Drip was shorter than the other girls, but in her eight-inch heels, she was the same height as Belle. Her face was done very pretty, and her smoky eye shadow, mixed with her long weave, gave her a mysterious look. She gave Belle a concerned look and ran her fingers through Belle's freshly flat-ironed hair.

"You cool?"

"Yes," Belle lied and then shook her head. "No. They're all looking at me like they want to—"

"Fuck you? Yeah, because they do. That's the part that you're supposed to use to your advantage."

"I know, but—"

"But nothing. Bitch, do you see all that money out there? These motherfuckers are more caked up that I even thought. We can all leave here with about five bands tonight. You want to make some of that, don't you?"

"Yes," Belle admitted. "I do. I just don't know where to start."

"Start with that nigga who asked you for a dance. We've been here for about thirty minutes, and he hasn't dropped a dime yet. And I can tell he's rolling in dough."

"How do you know that?"

"Because all of them out there are Black Card members. We only do parties for Black Card members. They have to pay ten thousand a month just in membership fees. They're the only ones who have access to these little home parties, as much cocaine as their noses can take, and if they submit their test results every month, they might even get their dicks wet. But don't worry, you don't have to do anything you aren't comfortable doing, boo. Feel special. Not all of the girls working for Gene get to be Gene's Girls. They're stuck working for an hourly wage at the club. But us? We are at the top of the food chain when it comes to this dancing shit. Seize the opportunity, girl!"

Belle turned her back on Drip and gave herself one last look in the mirror. It was too late to turn back at that point. She'd made the choice to dive off of into the deep end, and it was time to sink or swim.

"Okay," she said, turning back toward Drip. "How do I loosen up out there?"

"With this," Drip said and reached into her bra. She removed a small pill. "It's a Xanax. It will take the edge off."

Just as Belle was about to take it, the door to the bathroom pushed open. Both of the girls looked to see who was walking in on them, and they were both surprised to see Kidd. He looked from Drip to Belle and then back to Drip.

"Y'all have been gone for a hot second. Everything straight?"

"Yeah, we're cool," Belle said. She tried to hurry up and close her hand around the pill, but it was too late. He saw it.

"Ay, man, what the fuck is that?" he said and stepped all the way into the bathroom. He tried to make a grab for Belle's hand, but she snatched away.

"It's nothing," Belle tried to tell him.

"Yeah, it's just something to take the edge off," Drip said. "Relax. You know we all pop a pill from time to time."

"Yeah, but she ain't like y'all," Kidd said, glaring at Drip. "It's her first time doing this shit, and you're tryin'a have her out there all high and shit."

"Well, that's what you're here for, isn't it? To make sure nothing gets out of hand," Drip said and rolled her eyes at him.

Kidd clenched his jaw and turned back to Belle with his hand out. "Give me that shit, dude. You don't need it."

Belle almost gave it to him, but then she realized that was the first time he'd spoken to her after diving into her mind at the mall. He didn't care about her. He was just like the rest of the people in her life. There today, gone tomorrow.

"No," she said.

"What?"

"You heard me. I said no. I'm a grown-ass woman," she spat and tossed the pill to the back of her throat. "Now you can go back to not speaking to me. I'm one of Gene's Girls now. The only thing you need to do is protect me if one of these motherfuckers gets wrong. Other than that, stay the fuck away from me."

With that, Drip took Belle by the hand, and they left Kidd standing with a dumbfounded expression on his face. As Belle was walking, she felt the pill kicking in fast. Her entire body felt lighter, and suddenly, she was carefree. It was like she was drunk without the dizzy feeling, but her courage level had gone through the roof. The strobing lights in the darkness of the basement that at first intimidated her welcomed her that time. She snatched her hand away from Drip so that she could smack Luscious on the bottom as she walked by. She was in the middle of shaking what her mother gave her in one of the men's faces, and when she saw that the person who smacked her was Belle, she grinned.

"Okay, Nebraska. I see you must have gotten your shit together."

"Yeah, she's about to be feeling herself in a second," Drip said with a wink.

And feel herself she did. As she walked toward the man who had asked her for a dance, Belle rubbed herself seductively. He was sitting in a chair alone in a far corner, seemingly waiting for her.

"I thought you forgot about me," he said with a sly smile when she approached him.

"Me forget about something as handsome as you? Never, baby. What's your name?"

"Stephen."

"Well, Stephen, have you ever seen an ass this fat before?"

The words were coming out of her mouth, but she couldn't believe she was the one saying them. Gone was the timid girl who had walked in. She turned around to give him the perfect view of her apple bottom before she spread her legs and bent to grab her ankles. The music had slowed down by the time she walked out of the bathroom, so moving her body sensually to the beat was easy. She pulled out all of the tricks she'd seen exotic dancers do, and she tried her best to imitate them.

"Damn," she heard him say while she was on the carpet on her back with her legs open in the air.

She was shaking them so that he could see her meat wiggle, and he had the perfect view of her fat cat in her pink thong. The Xanax made the carpet beneath her feel so good on her skin that she wondered what else would feel good. And then she knew as soon as Stephen started throwing it. Money. He threw an entire stack on her body before she even stood back up, and when she did, he grabbed her hand gently, pulling her to him.

"I think I've thrown well over a hundred dollars," he said breathlessly. "Now come rub that fatty on my jimmy. Please."

Belle did as she was told without thinking twice. She put her hands on her knees as he leaned back into the leather chair he was in, and she twerked her bottom to the beat of whatever song was playing. She felt his hard-on between her cheeks, but she didn't care. She just wanted to keep feeling the money fall on her body. She realized the harder she bounced and ground down on him, the more he threw. She didn't bother picking up the money because Aria had told her it was security's job to sweep it up and put it in their individual piles to count at the end of the night. When Belle noticed that Stephen's hands fondled her backside for too long without throwing anything, she stopped dancing. It was time to find her next victim because Stephen's fantasy with Beauty was up.

"Hey, hey. Where are you going?" Stephen asked and grabbed Belle's arm. "We were just starting to have some fun."

"Fun stops when the money does," a voice said, coming up to them.

When Belle looked, she saw Kidd standing there, staring sternly at Stephen's hand on Belle's arm. Stephen instantly let Belle go, and she stepped away. Stephen smiled sheepishly and shrugged his shoulders up at Kidd.

"Hey, I pay my monthly dues like the rest of these fellas. You mean to tell me that I pay thousands of dollars a month and still have to throw dollars for a dance?"

"It's called a tip," Kidd told him. "This tour is a perk for only the best of Gene's clientele. You know that. Your monthly membership pays for access to that. Now if you want to cancel, be my guest. Otherwise, there are other girls who would appreciate the generosity you've shown Beauty tonight. There is also enough coke for you to take home to that pretty wife of yours."

Kidd nodded at Stephen's left finger, and he instantly balled his hand into a fist as if to hide it. Stephen cleared his throat as he stood up, and he went to join one of the other guys eyeballing Luscious, who was going bananas on the pole.

"Thank you," Belle said to Kidd and offered him a dopey smile.

"Shorty, let me talk to you for a minute," Kidd said to her and lightly grabbed her hand.

He led her to a back room away from the noisy party. He wanted to be able to speak to her without shouting over the music. When they were inside one of the basement bedrooms, Kidd turned the light on and closed the door.

"What's this? You wanted to get me all alone?" Belle grinned and leaned her body into him. She pressed her breasts on his chest and wrapped an arm around his neck. "You got some money in these pockets?"

Her free hand traveled down his leg, but instead of stopping at his pocket, she stopped at his crotch. The bulge there was impressive, and she licked her lips seductively up at him. He returned her look with one of longing before shaking his head and pulling away.

"Chill out. This ain't you, shorty," he said, focusing on her eyes. "I mean, look at you. You're high as a kite!"

"How can you tell me what is or isn't me? You barely even know me."

"True that, but I know this ain't you," Kidd said and pointed at her body. "I don't know if what happened back there at that gas station fucked you up or what, but you ain't gotta do this."

"Do what?"

"Use your body to make bread."

"What else am I going to do? This is just some quick cash until I get on my feet."

"Yeah, that's what they all said." Kidd shook his head. "Once you get in too deep, there ain't no getting out. And Gene . . ."

"Gene what?"

"He ain't gon' let you go. Especially when he sees you." There was a plea in his tone and his eyes at his last sentence.

He was trying to warn her, but Belle was so lit that she didn't care. The last person she let control her life was her father, and look where that got her. Broke and home-less. She rolled her eyes at Kidd and turned to go back out to the party, but he stopped her.

"Belle, please," he said. "I got you. Just stop doing this shit. I'll take care of you, I promise."

"Take care of me?" Belle scoffed and snatched her hand away. "I can take care of myself."

He wanted to stop her again, but instead, he let her leave the room. It seemed as if her mind was made up, and with the drug coursing through her system, there would be no getting through to her. Kidd knew one thing for certain: there was something about her that made him feel something dangerous. It was the same something that had almost made him put a bullet between dude's eyes for snatching her arm. It was the same something that could mess up his own paper, and that was why he couldn't stay there. He couldn't watch Belle destroy her-self while everyone else celebrated her. No, he would let her do that by herself.

In the next room, there was a party with only two peo-ple going on. While the other girls were busy entertaining their guests, Aria had cornered one of her very own. His name was Jeremy Jeter, and he was the senior vice president of a software company. His take-home salary alone was enough to knock the panties off most women, but that didn't mean he didn't mind paying for pussy. He also had a bit of a gambling problem, and that didn't go over too well with most ladies.

"Hell yeah, take it off," he said from where he sat on the bed.

The lighting in the room was dim, and he'd removed the jacket he was wearing as if it had suddenly gotten hot in there. His hands moved back and forth on his thighs like a kid in a toy section after his mother told him not to touch anything. His eyes were glued to Aria as she swayed her body to the music coming from under the closed bedroom door. Not only was she a temptress, but Aria had a way of putting all her clients in a trance. She was the tamer, and Jeremy was her snake. She pouted her red lips as she walked seductively toward the bed with her hand behind her back.

"Are you ready to have some real fun?" she asked and ran her finger down his chest.

"Does it involve me getting my dick sucked?" he asked breathily.

"Now, now. There will be plenty of time for all of that," Aria answered. "Be patient. In fact, I brought my whole bag of goodies in here just for you. Let's have some fun, shall we?"

She took her hand from behind her back and revealed that she was holding two pairs of handcuffs. When he saw them, he quickly showed his pearly whites and lay back on the bed so that his head was on one of the pillows. He then held his arms out, letting her know that he was okay with whatever fun she had planned for him.

"Make me feel good, baby," he said as she handcuffed him to the bed.

"Oh, I will," she said and walked over to the bag by the door. "This is going to be a time you'll never forget."

From the bag, she grabbed two black scarves so that she could tie his legs down as well. When she was positive that he couldn't get loose, she grabbed a few more things from her bag and climbed on top of him seductively. She moved her hips as she ground down on his erection and watched the look of pure bliss take over his face. He began to moan, so she placed in his mouth the gag ball she'd brought with her, and she tied it at the back of his head.

"Do you like that?" she asked, grinding harder.

He nodded ferociously.

"I know you like that. You wish you could feel this pussy on your raw dick, don't you?"

He nodded again, that time with a muffled moan.

"Mmm, I know, baby. Do you know what I like?"

He shook his head. His eyes were too busy looking at her exposed nipples to see the flash of the blade being put to his throat.

"I like it when you pay Gene his motherfucking money on time," she said, pressing the sharp knife to his throat. "Now why the fuck did you think it was okay to show your face at this party, Jeremy, when you've missed your last three payments? Did you think Gene was going to let you keep enjoying the amenities without you playing your part?"

Under her, Jeremy tried to fight against his restraints, but she had him tied up too good. Next, he tried to yell, perhaps to get help, but that was no use either. No one could hear him. Aria feigned a yawn at his futile attempts until finally, he stopped.

"Realize you're not getting free until I allow it, eh?" she said with a chuckle. "Now let's get back to business, shall we? From what I hear, you have a little bit of a gambling problem. So I take it you know all about choices and options. Well, I have a few options for you to choose from. I can kill you right now on this bed, slice your throat open, and watch your blood spill out all over this nice thirty-five-year-old body. Or you can pay Gene what you owe him right here, right now, and you can continue to enjoy the party. What do you say?"

Jeremy glared up at Aria, and he screamed until his face turned red. The rage he felt read all over his face, but that was the least of Aria's concerns. To her, he was as scary as a mouse. Gene was the boogeyman in comparison. The only thing on her mind was doing as he said, which was collecting all debts from his clients while she was on tour. Jeremy was in the hole $20,000, yet hadn't missed a party and had even shown up at the Bliss Lounge in Miami. She was prepared to do whatever it took to recover the money, even if it meant cutting him into tiny little pieces.

When he was done screaming, he panted for air. Aria waited to speak again until she saw the defeated look in his eyes.

"The clock is ticking. You have five seconds to make a decision. Actually, make that one." She pressed the knife harder to his neck, and he shook his head.

"Mmm!" he moaned and made a small gesture with his head toward his right pants pocket. "Mmm!"

Her eyes followed the gesture and saw a small bulge there. She reached inside the pocket and pulled out his wallet and his phone. The wallet only had about $1,000 in twenties inside of it. She pressed the phone to one of his thumbs, and it unlocked instantly.

"That's the funny thing about technology. Everything is literally at our fingertips. These days you can transfer money all over the world, all from your phone. Isn't that convenient? Ah, here we go."

In less than thirty seconds, using his fingerprint again, she transferred all the money that was owed to Gene from Jeremy's checking account. When Aria was done, she gently slid the phone back in his pocket along with his wallet and stood up.

"I can't lie. I'm a little disappointed, Jeremy," she said as she strutted to the door. "I thought you would put up a little more fight than that. But no matter. I got what I wanted. I'll have Phil come in here and untie you momentarily. Oh, and I wouldn't try any funny business if I were you. I have a knife, but Phil? He has a gun. Enjoy the rest of the party!"

She winked back at him before grabbing her bag of goodies and tucking her knife back into one of the sides. When she opened the bedroom door, sure enough, Phil was standing guard outside of it.

"You handle your business?"

"Always," she said with a smile and walked away to join the rest of the girls.

The first thing she saw was Luscious shaking her gigantic booty and a shower of bills being thrown at it. The second thing Aria saw was Belle in the corner, smiling in the face of a man and him giving her a handful of hundreds. All she had to do was smile and she was raking in dough. Gene was going to love her the moment he met her. Aria knew it. She just hadn't decided yet if that was a good thing or a bad thing.

Chapter 6

My right hand is a monster.
—Deontay Wilder

"Where are you off to?"

Aria's voice caught Kidd off guard, but he didn't stop what he was doing. It was the morning after the party and the other girls were still sound asleep in the hotel. Kidd had gotten up to go outside to the bus before the sun was in the sky. He'd removed all of his things and relocated them to the trunk of Belle's car. Everything of hers that had been inside it that he thought she would need he'd put on the tour bus. He didn't give Aria eye contact when he shut the trunk and went to the driver's side door.

"I'm just gon' meet y'all back in Miami," he answered. "Gene will send somebody to the next stop to replace me as security when he knows I'm gone."

"Why are you leaving us so suddenly?"

Kidd bit the inside of his cheek and hit the top of the Camaro lightly with his fist before finally looking her way. She was wearing a thin pair of leggings, a pair of boots, and a light jacket. Her hair was wrapped up in a scarf, but her makeup from the previous night was still sitting perfectly on her face.

"You should go back inside," he told her. "It's cold out here. We don't need you getting sick now, do we?"

"No, what I don't need is Belle filing a police report on you for stealing her car."

"Not stealing, borrowing. You and I both know she's not gon' give a fuck about this car now that she has y'all. Plus it will be waiting for her when the bus gets back to Miami."

"Whatever," Aria said, crossing her arms. "You still never said why you're leaving. You've always been our security on the tours."

"Yeah, well, things change."

"Things like . . . Belle?" Aria raised her eyebrow at him, and when his jaw clenched, she knew she'd hit the nail on the head.

"She's not built for this life, and you know it."

"I mean, she brought in four thousand dollars on her own last night. I'd say she's a natural."

"That's not what I mean." Kidd clenched his fists and sighed. "Did you even think to look her up? When we found her at that gas station, did you even think to look up who she was?"

"Nooo," Aria said and made a face. "We've found girls in raunchier places than a gas station bathroom."

"Well, I looked her up. It just seemed odd to me that a girl her age could be riding around in a brand-new Camaro but claim to be broke."

"You mean she's not broke?"

"She is now, but she wasn't before. Nowhere near it. Her father was Lucas Dubois, owner of a major management company. He was murdered along with his wife and son, leaving her with nothing. Not even his estate."

"So what's wrong with her making a little bit of money?"

"She ain't like us, man! When you look at her, you see a dollar. When I look at her, I see something more. She's supposed to be in college studyin' for class. Instead, you got her out here popping pussy like you."

"And what's wrong with me?"

"You know what's wrong with you! And me! You know how Gene is, just like I do. This ain't freedom. It's a prison. Even when she saves enough money to get out, she won't be able to leave. And if she tries to, you know what will happen. Because it happened to you."

"You're wrong," Aria said to him, trying to hide the fact that his words had gotten to her.

"If you really believed that, you wouldn't be standing there looking like you have shit under your nose. I'm out!"

He threw up two fingers before getting in the car and driving away. When he looked in the rearview, he saw Aria walking back in the hotel, probably to tell the others that he was leaving. He hoped that Belle wouldn't report her car stolen while he was on the highway, but then again, he didn't care. He had to get away, far away, from all of them.

There was a long road ahead of him, but he passed the time with music and getting lost in his own thoughts. He'd meant what he said. Belle wasn't built for what was in store for her. She had been raised with a silver spoon in her mouth while he and Aria had been raised on the streets. They had been raised to do whatever it took to survive, but for Belle, it was different. Pain was pushing her in the wrong direction, and Kidd could see that clear as day.

As he drove, trying to beat the morning traffic, Kidd reflected on the day that Gene took him in. It was a hot summer night, and Kidd was only 16 at the time. It was a day that he wished he could go back and change, but of course, he couldn't.

"Kidd, come on! Let's go!"

"Nah! I think he's about to stick his dick in her butt!"

Two young kids had been standing on red crates outside of a bedroom window. They had been peering inside until one of them, Ollie, checked the time on his watch. When he saw that it read after ten o'clock, he'd jumped down and taken off toward the sidewalk. He stopped only because he noticed that his friend was not behind him.

"Come on! We're gon' get caught watchin' Mrs. Hansen fuckin' again!"

"Better us than her husband," Kidd said with a grin and peeked back inside the window just as Mrs. Hansen arched her back.

Mrs. Hansen was the prettiest woman on their block. She had chocolate skin, long hair, a pretty face, and a fat, old behind. Everybody said that Mr. Hansen was a lucky man to have such a nice-looking wife, but Mr. Hansen didn't know that while he was at work, different men were in and out of his house. Kidd felt himself get hard when Mrs. Hansen buried her head in her pillow and parted her butt cheeks so the young fellow behind her could penetrate her. Right when Mrs. Hansen's hand began to clench the sheets, Kidd was snatched away from the window.

"Hey, man, what the fuck is your problem?"

"My problem is my mom is gon' kill us if we're late again."

"Oh, shit, what time is it?"

"Ten fifteen!"

"*Shit, let's go,*" *Kidd said, forgetting all about Mrs. Hansen getting her back blown out.*

He hopped down, and the boys took off running down the street toward their home. When the Feds had come and taken Kidd's mom away the prior year for money laundering, Ollie's mom, Sherell, took him in. She'd been Kidd's neighbor for years and refused to let him get lost in the system, especially since he had been her son's best friend since the two were in diapers. What she hadn't counted on was having such a big load on her shoulders raising two teenagers. At 16, both Ollie and Kidd often had their noses in mischief. It had gotten to the point where Sherell had to give them a ten thirty curfew. If they ever missed it, that meant no video games for a week, and their games were life for them in the summertime.

"*Yeah, get y'all bad asses home!*" *a voice shouted at them as they pushed their legs as fast as they would go.*

"*Fuck you, Rodney!*" *Ollie shouted back at the old man smoking a blunt on his porch.*

Kidd flicked him off as they passed his house, and he heard Rodney laughing behind them. It was dark out, but the boys could find their way home with their eyes closed. They knew the neighborhood like the back of their hands. It took them five minutes to reach the small one-story house, and they saw that the kitchen light was on. That meant one thing, and one thing only. Sherell was in there watching the clock on the oven like a hawk mentally daring them to miss curfew. They were laughing when they burst through the back door to see Sherell exactly where they knew she would be: sitting at the high-top wooden table, facing the oven.

"*Look at you! Ready to raise hell!*" *Ollie joked and wrapped his arms around her.*

"*Yeah, you couldn't wait to yell at us,*" *Kidd said and grinned at her.*

She pushed Ollie away from her and didn't say anything. The look on her face was just flat-out indifferent, which was strange for her. Normally her lips spread from ear to ear when she saw them, but that night she didn't smile. In fact, she looked sad.

"*Ma, what's wrong?*" *Ollie asked, taking notice of her lack of energy.*

She ignored him and looked straight at Kidd. Just looking into his eyes caused tears to form into her own, and he didn't understand why she was so sad.

"*What's wrong?*" *Kidd asked and touched her arm.*

"*I'm sorry, Kidd. I tried,*" *she said and sniffled.* "*I tried.*"

"*What do you mean you tried? Tried what?*"

"*To keep you,*" *she answered.* "*The courts are terminating my guardianship.*"

"*But w . . . why?*"

"*Your next of kin has stepped up and said that they want you.*"

"*Who?*"

"*Your uncle Gene.*"

"*Uncle Gene?*" *Kidd scoffed.* "*I don't know that nigga.*"

"*Hey! Watch your mouth in this house, young man!*" *Sherell snapped.* "*Sometimes the cards the Lord deals us aren't the ones that we see fitting. He will be here to get you in the morning, so you'll need to pack your things tonight. But, Kidd, you know you're always welcome to come—*"

"*This is bullshit!*" *Kidd cut her off and knocked the salt shaker off the table.*

He stormed from the kitchen and went to the room that he shared with Ollie. He fell on the bed that Sherell had bought for him, the one that he figured would be his until he graduated high school. Life had been good, given the circumstances. Sherell was good to him, and he had known her since his earliest memories. Why did his Uncle Gene all of a sudden want him? His mom had been away for a year, and he hadn't heard a word from her family.

All he knew about his uncle Gene was that he was his mother Annette's older, rich brother who lived across town, the same rich brother who never helped them out. Annette had been working two jobs, and still she'd not been able to make ends meet. She ended up having to do some unethical things to pay some bills and got caught up in the long run. If Gene had just lent a hand to help his baby sister out, then maybe she wouldn't have been sent to jail.

Kidd hit his head back on the pillow and thought about running away. He quickly put that thought in the back of his head. They would just find him, because where would he go? He had no people and no money.

"Hey, man," Ollie said, entering the room and sitting on the edge of his own bed. "Kidd?"

"What's up?" Kidd finally answered, staring at the ceiling.

"Regardless of whatever, you're still my brother."

"This is still bullshit," Kidd said.

"I know, but it is what it is. Moms said dude is rich as hell."

"Somethin' like that."

"So that means you'll be straight," Ollie said, trying to look on the brighter side of things.

"My mom woulda been straight too if he had just helped us out. Why the nigga want me now?"

"I don't know the answer to that. But, Kidd?"

"Yeah."

"Don't make this harder on Ma than it already is," Ollie said, and Kidd finally looked him in the eyes. *"She's really hurt out there. You know she's always loved you like a son. Shit, sometimes I think she likes you more than she likes me."*

Kidd couldn't help the grin that spread on his face. Ollie held his hand out, and Kidd sat up to shake it.

"Brothers," Ollie said.

"Forever," Kidd said back and gripped Ollie's hand tight.

The next morning came faster than Kidd expected, but he'd done as Sherell asked and packed all of his things. When the doorbell rang, Kidd was sitting in the living room on the couch beside Ollie and Sherell with his suitcase next to him. Sherell got up and opened the door, and the way Gene walked through the doors was something Kidd would never forget. For one, the Gucci suit he had on had to cost a couple thousand dollars. Same with the Gucci frames on his face. He had a hairline so sharp that you would probably cut your finger if you tried to touch it. Two big men had entered the house as well and stood a few steps behind Gene with their hands at their sides. One of them was holding a suitcase in his hand. Kidd was so shocked at the scene that he and Ollie looked at each other with wide eyes.

"You must be Sherell," Gene said, taking his shades off. He then took her hand in his and brought it to his lips. *"I can't thank you enough for looking after my nephew after all this time. I would have come to get him sooner, but I had too much going on in my life at the time."*

"Y . . . you're welcome?" Sherell said, obviously as taken aback as the boys.

Gene made a motion with one of his hands, and instantly, the man holding the briefcase handed it to him. With a smile, Gene held it out for her to see. When he opened it, Sherell's hand instantly went to her chest. The briefcase was packed neatly with nothing but hundred-dollar bills. She shook her head.

"I . . . I can't," she told him.

"I insist. For your troubles," he told her and closed the briefcase. "In fact, I won't take no for an answer. A beautiful woman like you deserves every penny inside. Now, where is that nephew of mine?"

He set the briefcase next to Sherell's feet and moved around her as if he weren't a guest in her house. His eyes went right over Ollie and straight to Kidd. Gene gave him a once-over before smiling big and opening his arms for a hug. Kidd just looked at him before he stood up and grabbed his suitcase.

"I'll be in the car," Kidd said. "What you pull up in, a limo?"

He turned to Ollie, who was grinning at his joke, and slapped hands with him.

"Be easy, boy," Ollie told him. "You know where I'll be at."

"No doubt," Kidd said, and the boys embraced briefly.

Next Kidd turned to face Sherell. He could tell that she was trying hard not to cry, but he thought back to what Ollie said the night before and put a fake smile on his face.

"You know I'ma visit, Mama Rell," he said and gave her a big hug. "Fix that long face."

"I'm going to miss you, boy," Sherell said, holding him tight and rocking side to side. "You better not forget about us small folk."

"Never," he said, pulling away and planting a kiss on her forehead. "Plus I am small folk."

With his suitcase in tow, he exited the house and walked toward an all-black Cadillac Escalade that was parked on the street. He heard the door shut behind him, and before he'd made it to the truck, he felt an arm on his shoulder.

"Andrew, I know this might be an awkward transition for you, but I assure you that you will like your new life. You're sixteen now, right? We can go look at cars later today. How does that sound?"

"Kidd."

"What?"

"My name is Kidd," Kidd said and glared at his uncle. "And money can't buy my love. You shoulda tried that with my mom."

He snatched his shoulder away and continued down the concrete walkway to where Gene's security already stood waiting with the back door open. They took his suitcase, and he hopped in the back seat, shutting the door before Gene could try to get in on his side. He knew he was acting like a child throwing a temper tantrum, but he didn't care. He was mad, and hiding that was impossible. The ride to Gene's luxury home in Miami Beach was just like the next two weeks of Kidd's life: long.

Gene's gigantic eight-bedroom, five-bathroom mansion took some getting used to, especially since Kidd was so accustomed to the tiny two-bedroom house he'd shared with Sherell and Ollie. Gene's home came complete with a pool and a tennis court. But as much as he was blown away, he was disgusted. Gene tried connect to Kidd, he even tried to give him money to go shopping, but Kidd wouldn't accept any of it. He just couldn't get over the fact that Gene had been living like a king across town while he and his mother lived like peasants barely surviving. He would be 17 in less than a month, and that meant he'd only have to endure living with his uncle for a year before he could leave.

Besides the lavishness of the home, there were a few things about it that stood out to Kidd. One was that each entrance was guarded by a security guard. Another was that there was surveillance all over the place. It was a fact that Gene was a wealthy man, but the question arose of how exactly he got all his riches.

Gene had given Kidd access to the entire house, but the basement was off-limits. For a while, Kidd respected his wishes, but after months of seeing his uncle disappear down there with his minions, curiosity got the best of him. He took notice of the fact that whenever Gene was down there, Kidd couldn't hear a thing no matter how quiet the house was.

The night that he decided to break the rule was the same night Gene walked through the door with a man Kidd had never seen before. Behind each of them was their own three-man entourage following closely behind. Both gentlemen were dressed in dapper attire as if they'd just left a fancy dinner, and they had big smiles on their faces. Kidd had been in the large living room, lying on the couch and half paying attention to the music videos playing on the television when he heard them walking past toward the basement door. When Kidd sat up, Gene motioned a hand toward him.

"Percy, let me introduce you to my nephew. This is Kidd. My dear sister got herself locked up, and he will be staying with me for a while. Kidd, say hello to Percy."

"What's up," Kidd said and gave the man a nod.

He couldn't quite get the guy's angle. Percy was the same height as his uncle. Although in a suit, the man had a roughness about him. His skin was the color of honey, and his facial hair was neatly trimmed, as was the low-cut hair on his head. He rocked a diamond chain on his neck that spelled out the word "God" on it. Kidd's eyes went to the man's hands and saw that his knuckles were scarred over like his fists had seen quite a few fights in their day.

"Kidd? What kind of name is that?" Percy asked with a tinge of humor in his voice.

"What kind of name is Percy?" Kidd shot back.

"Touché, young man, touché," Percy said with a smile. *It was coy, and the way his lips spread reminded Kidd of a snake. "I once asked my mother that question, and you know what she told me, boy?"*

"What?"

"She told me that when I was born, she knew I would be a savage. That I wouldn't take anything from anybody, just like her. For that, she named me Perseus, after the powerful demigod." Percy's chest bumped out slightly, and Gene smirked beside him. "And she was right. These hands have seen more street battles than the number of your age, here where I was raised and in other territories. They have never seen a loss. Only victory. I assume that's why your uncle has invited me here today."

"Where is your mother now?" Kidd asked.

"Unlike your mother, she was graced with death before lockup," Percy answered and flashed his teeth again. *"No offense."*

"None taken." Kidd shrugged. "In fact, in that whole speech, all I heard you say was that Perseus is your real name. With a name and face like that, you probably never get any pussy."

The men standing behind Gene chuckled a little bit, but the ones behind Percy kept stony faces. The corner of Percy's lip twitched along with his hands, but he did not make a move. Instead, he smoothed out his suit and turned to Gene.

"It would do you some good to teach your nephew some manners while he is here."

"Duly noted," Gene said and motioned toward the basement door. "Now to attend to business."

Percy shot Kidd a glare before he went to the basement door. Gene followed him, but before he did, he glanced back at Kidd and gave Kidd a look. Not knowing what it meant, Kidd watched all of the men disappear until he heard the basement door shut behind them. He tried to go back to watching music videos, but he was no longer interested in watching women shake their rear ends in swimsuits. Something that Percy said had made its way back into his mind.

"I'm assuming that's why your uncle invited me here today."

What had Percy meant by that? And what use did Gene have for a street soldier anyways? Those questions were what led Kidd to open the door to the basement. He stood at the top, staring at the wide, carpeted stairs, debating if he wanted to take the risk of being caught. Curiosity got the best of him when he heard nothing. The lights were on, but he didn't hear one voice or foot shuffle. Where had they gone?

He took one step down. Then another, and then another, until he was completely in the basement. At the sight of what was down there, instantly, his breath caught. He didn't know what he expected to see. Maybe some furniture and a huge television on the wall. Some rooms and even a kitchen, but none of that was here. To the right of him, there was nothing but dry wall painted a nice cocaine white. To the left and about ten feet away from him were double doors leading to what looked to be a large room. A little ways in front of him was a gun range, an actual gun range inside of the house, which explained why Kidd never heard any sounds coming from the basement. The walls and windows must have been soundproof. The area Kidd was standing in looked to be a lobby, complete with a glass table and two nice, cushioned chairs. He found himself wondering if the magazines on the table were current.

As Kidd walked toward the glass windows on the gun range, he prepared to open the door to get a better look at the guns hanging from the wall to the side, but a noise caught his attention. It wasn't loud, and it sounded like a deep belly laugh. Swiveling his head, he saw that one of the double doors to the room was slightly cracked. He forgot all about the gun range and quietly went to the door so that he could peek in.

As it turned out, the room was an office. Gene's office. Kidd now knew why his uncle would be down there for so long. He couldn't see the entire room, but from the looks of it, the office was as luxurious as the rest of the house. On each end of his long desk, there were two tall vases that reminded Kidd of the ones he'd seen in the movie Rush Hour 2. *Gene sat at his desk with his elbows atop it and his hands gently clasped together as he stared at*

Percy. Gene's men stood beside him, while Percy's stood beside him on the opposite side of the desk. Kidd couldn't tell which one of them had laughed, but he strained his ears to hear what was being said without accidently nudging the door open more.

"My offer amuses you?" Gene asked.

"Man, you just asked me to be security for a titty bar," Percy said and shook his head. "Your name holds weight in the streets. You have power out here, and you mean you want to give that up to become some kind of pimp?"

"The Bliss Lounge will not be your typical titty bar," Gene replied calmly. "In fact, it will be far from that."

"You're talking some elite shit. And I'll be the first to tell you that niggas don't spend that kind of cash on pussy when they can get it for free."

"I didn't ask you here for you to scrutinize my revolutionary idea. I put an offer on the table, and now I am waiting for your answer. The success of the club isn't your concern as long as I am paying you."

"How you gon' pay me if ain't no money rolling in? And if you ain't selling dope no more, where you gon' get the kind of cash that's on this paper? See, you're asking me to leave guaranteed paper to hop on board for this little trial run you have up your sleeve."

"And if it's a success? Then what?"

"Pay whoever your security detail is in pennies, because I'm telling you, ain't no money in what you're trying to do, G. Shit, people already have KOD and Magic City. Fuck they need a Bliss Lounge for?"

"I'm sure I don't need to remind you who you're speaking to, so it will be wise for you to correct your tone."

"Yeah, okay." Percy laughed again. "This business meeting is over. My answer isn't just no. It's a hell no,

*and I'm going to forgive you for wasting my time. I just
came to see if what the streets were saying was true."*

"And what's that?"

*"That you're losing your grip on the streets. And now I
know for myself that you're giving up all your power for
some pussy. What a fuckin' joke," Percy said and spat on
Gene's desk. "Let's go, y'all."*

*He stood up to leave, but Gene's voice stopped him.
"I'm afraid to inform you that you are wrong."*

"What?"

"You're wrong."

"I just call it like I see it."

*"You see only with your eyes, and that's the problem,"
Gene chuckled. "See, I gave up the game a long time ago.
My hands haven't touched a brick in years because I have
young, dumb niggas like you willing to do all of the dirty
work for me. I've always been smart enough to know
that the life of a kingpin ends only in one of two ways,
and we both know what those are. Eventually, everyone
gets caught up in the life. I decided to bow out gracefully
while I'm still hitting high. I've decided to go mostly legit,
and I've just offered you the job of a lifetime. You just spit
that back in my face, and while I will let you walk out
of here with breath still in your body, I will never forget
this day. Understand? And one more thing: there ain't no
power in this world greater than pussy."*

*"Yeah, whatever, nigga. Just know that when you fall,
Perseus will be here to take your place."*

*"Dexter, please show Percy the door," Gene instructed
one of the men standing beside him.*

*Percy turned his back on Gene and walked toward the
double doors. It happened so quick that Kidd didn't have
time to make a break for the stairs. When Percy pulled*

open the cracked door all the way, he caught Kidd standing there like a deer in headlights.

"Nosy ass," he said to Kidd and bumped past him.

Kidd tried to step to the side, but it was too late. His uncle had already seen him there. Kidd couldn't describe the expression that crossed Gene's face, but it wasn't a pleasant one. Dexter followed closely behind Perseus and his entourage. Kidd didn't know whether he should go back upstairs too. After a few moments of just standing there, he turned his back and tried to quickly go up to his room.

"No, you stay," *Gene said from his desk.* "You two go."

He gave the men beside them their leave, and they didn't wait for a second instruction. When they were gone, Gene waved for Kidd to come into the office and sit down. Once seated, Kidd waited for his uncle to give him a stern talking-to. Imagine his surprise when those words never came and, in fact, it was quite the contrary.

"I imagine you were standing out there the entire time."

"Not the entire time, sir. Just part of it. Maybe most of it. You mad at me?"

"I don't know yet. What made you come down here when I specifically told you that the basement is off-limits to you?"

"I guess I ain't never been good at following rules. And I guess I wasn't really thinking. Or maybe I was thinking. About what you were doing down here and why some random people got to see what was here and I couldn't."

"And what are you thinking now?"

"That Percy is an asshole."

Gene surprised Kidd with a hearty laugh. When he had gotten it all out, he nodded in agreement with his nephew. "You're right about that."

"I can't believe you asked him to be security. He's a little too lippy for all that. He's the type of nigga . . . I mean, man I wouldn't even want too close to my business," Kidd said, looking into his uncle's eyes.

"I'm starting to realize that. There is nothing more worrisome than a man afraid of change. That kind of man doesn't make good for the rise of business and is your worst enemy once you reach the top. Still, I'm at a loss when it comes to a security detail, and I'm trying to get the ball rolling by next month."

"I heard Percy say that you were opening a gentlemen's club?"

"Something like that."

"Oh," was all Kidd said.

Gene raised his eyebrow at him. *"You sneak down here and eavesdrop on a conversation that you have no business listening to in the first place, but now you choose to bite your tongue. Speak, boy."*

"I'm just saying, from what I pieced together, now I have a good idea of what you do to live like this. I mean, I think I knew already. You're some kind of kingpin, huh?"

"Maybe."

"Well, let's just say that you are. You mean to tell me you're going to give up your throne to open up a titty bar? That just doesn't make sense, Unc."

"You're starting to sound a lot like Percy."

"Nah, he was telling you. I'm asking. Why give up everything for that?"

"Maybe my eyes are open just a little wider than of those around me. What are people addicted to the most besides money? Women and drugs. Combine the two and you rule the world. Why settle for being a king when you can be a god?"

"You're going to push weight through the club?"

"Even better," Gene said with a smile. *"And when you're older, I may decide to go into more detail, but for now I'll settle for teaching you how to shoot a gun. Come on, let me show how to hold a pistol."*

"I know how to hold a pistol," Kidd said.

"I mean how to hold it so that you never miss," Gene said, standing up from his chair.

"Yeah," Kidd said and followed his uncle to the gun range. *"Then maybe I can be your security. That way we can keep the money in the family."*

The younger voice of himself faded in Kidd's mind as he pulled into the parking garage of his condo back at home. The drive had been a long one, but his memory had kept him company. He hadn't even known it back then, but he spoke his future into existence. Not only did he grow up to be one of the Bliss Lounge's best security details, but he was also one of the best shooters in the state. After Kidd graduated, Gene had hired military personnel to train him not only in the art of shooting, but in combat as well. Kidd was literally a walking weapon, and Gene used him to the best of his ability.

When Kidd walked into his home, he noticed that everything was exactly how he left it. He called the place his bachelor pad, and despite the short amount of time he spent there, he enjoyed it. Almost everything inside was white—the walls, the countertops, the couch, and everything in his bedroom—because he liked the purity of it all. There was a cleaner who came once a week, so his place stayed pretty neat and tidy.

Upon entering, he took his shoes off and left them by the door. The first thing he wanted to do was take a shower. The second thing he wanted to do was lie in his bed, but of course, that was just too much like right. The second he turned on the water in the tub of the master bathroom, his phone began to vibrate violently against his leg in his pocket.

"Hello?"

"Aria told me that you've come home."

Kidd recognized his uncle's voice instantly. He of course knew that Gene would find out he was back in town sooner or later. Kidd was just thinking that it would be later. He was hoping to get at least a few hours to himself.

"Yeah, I just walked through the doors."

"Everything all right, nephew? Why did you leave the tour?"

"Yeah," Kidd said, thinking about Belle. "Everything is all right."

"Is everything going good with the tour? How did the new girl do on her first night?"

"Everything was everything, Unc," Kidd said, not really wanting to recap the night at all. "Let's just say there were no complaints."

"Good, that's what I like to hear. Still, I would have rather you waited until the tour was over to come back home."

"I was just gon' to have one of the others replace me for the rest of the tour, that's all. I needed a break."

There was a long pause on the other end of the phone.

"I guess I'm so used to working you so hard I don't realize that you don't get too many breaks," Gene said finally.

"Life is a constant revolving circle. I just thought I'd hit pause for a second before I come back into the office."

"Well, since you're home, you'll have the opportunity to take a break once you do one little thing for me. That's why I'm calling, I have a job for you. I need you to meet me at my house in the morning."

"All right," Kidd answered because he couldn't say no if he wanted to. "What's the job?"

"Remember our old friend Perseus?"

Chapter 7

If you are curious, you'll find the puzzles around you. If you are determined, you will solve them.
                                    —Erno Rubik

Knock! Knock!

The wooden door was hard underneath Kidd's knuckles when he knocked, but he was sure somebody heard him with as hard as he'd hit the door. As he stood outside the house his uncle had brought him to so long ago, he enjoyed the feel of the humid air and the warm sun on the back of his neck. The day was still warming up, but sixty degrees still felt better than what the Midwest had to offer, and he had to admit that he was happy to be home.

After waiting a few minutes and getting no response, Kidd raised his hand to knock on the door again. Right before his fist hit the door, he stopped because something dawned on him. He had a key. Shaking his head at himself for being so airheaded, he pulled out his keys and let himself inside.

Nothing was different about the home, but of course it wouldn't be. Gene was good with change everywhere else, but he liked his home to remain the same. It even smelled the same, like clean linen and laundry. No lights in the home were on, but the natural light from the sun lit the entire home up, and Kidd found himself smiling to himself as he stood in the foyer. He had truly gone from a pauper to a prince. A prince who had to earn his keep, but a prince nonetheless.

"Unc!" Kidd called up the spiral staircase to the left of him. "Unc!"

When nobody answered him, he pulled his phone from his pocket and called Gene's phone. It rang twice before the line was picked up.

"Good morning, nephew."

"Good morning? I thought you told me to come by this morning."

"I did, didn't I?" Gene asked, and Kidd couldn't help but notice that something about his tone sounded a little off. "Are you at the house already?"

"Uh, yeah."

"Well, hang out for a while. I'm going to be some hours."

"Where's Maria?" Kidd asked, looking around for Gene's housekeeper. "I was at the door, knocking, and nobody answered."

"You don't have your key?"

"I remembered I had it after nobody answered the door."

"I had to let Maria go. She was getting old and kept staining my laundry. She's back with her family now."

"Oh. Well, everything still looks good," Kidd said, walking around the house and noticing how neat everything was.

"I'm not incompetent, my dear nephew. I know how to keep up my home."

"Yeah, yeah. Where are you at anyway?"

"Just out handling some last-minute business," was all Gene said.

"Like what?"

"Nothing that you need to concern your head with. For what I need you to do, I need your mind clear and for you to be at full strength. Don't worry about me, my dear boy. I'll see you soon."

"Yeah, all right. I'll see you later then."

They hung up the phone without saying goodbye, and Kidd sighed. If he had thought to call Gene before he left his own place, he would be still asleep in his bed. However, instead of wallowing in his own annoyance, Kidd figured he'd better make every hour count. There was nothing worse to him than wasted time, so he headed toward the basement. He decided then that he would get some shots in while he waited for Gene to get back.

Except he never made it to the range. When his foot touched the floor in the basement, he had every intention of going straight to find the gun he wanted to shoot with that day. However, fate had other plans for him. He noticed that one of the doors to Gene's office was wide open and he was looking directly at Gene's desk. He was about to just shut the door, but then curiosity got the best of him.

He eased closer and closer to the desk before sitting down in Gene's chair, a place where his uncle spent most of his idle time. It was a comfortable chair, Kidd had to admit while his eyes traveled the room, seeing it the way that Gene did. He smoothed his hands along the top of the shiny, smooth desktop and found himself admiring the craftmanship. There were three horizontal drawers on the right, and there was one that stood out to him. The second drawer had a turned key in it. Gene must have been in the middle of something, because the drawer wasn't all the way shut. It had gotten caught on some papers seemingly stuffed inside.

Kidd knew that Gene hated for anyone to go through his things, but his hand was itching to pull open the drawer. Gene had acted strange on the phone, and Kidd couldn't help but wonder why. Not only that, but Gene never said he was going to be somewhere and then wasn't there. It just wasn't like him to not be at the house when he told Kidd to be there. Something had to be up. Something important.

Before he talked himself out of it, the drawer was open, and the papers were in his hands. Only they weren't papers. They were photographs, and when he saw who they were of, his eyebrow raised. Looking up at him in a frozen frame was the woman he'd just had to force himself to leave. Belle. But why did Gene have her pictures in his drawer? He turned one of them over, and his eyes widened at the words he saw: "Find her."

Confused wasn't the word to describe what he was feeling. He rummaged around the desk some more in hopes of finding an answer of some sort, but he found nothing. The only way for Kidd to figure out exactly why Gene was looking for Belle was to ask him or stand close enough to him to figure it out. He put the pictures back in the drawer and shut it exactly how he found it. His phone rang from his pocket, and he quickly pulled it out to see who it was.

"What up, my boy?" he answered.

"So, niggas touch down in the city and just don't say shit, huh?" Kidd's childhood best friend Ollie said into the phone.

"Man, it's not even like that," Kidd said with a grin. "How'd you even know I was back?"

"You know I always check on your spot when you're gone, boy. You really need to learn how to make your bed up. You're too old for all that."

"You know what? Fuck you," Kidd said.

"I got a bitch for that," Ollie retorted. "Where you at anyways?"

"At Gene's spot. He told me to meet him here, but he ain't here yet. You tryin'a come shoot around with me until he get here?"

"And what? Embarrass you?"

"Nigga, you ain't gon' embarrass shit," Kidd said, laughing out loud.

"Yeah, yeah. I'm on the way."

Bzzzzz!

The loud buzzer was something that Gene would never get used to or like. He couldn't decide whether that or the hard plastic chair he was sitting in was the most irritating part of the place, the "place" being Lowell Correctional Institution, a women's prison. The only good thing about the buzzer was that it signified when the guard had finally brought his sister in to sit with him.

He watched as the big, burly guard guided her to the chair across from him at the metal table. She looked good despite the dull prison uniform she was wearing. The top of her jumpsuit was tied around her waist, and the white T-shirt she wore showed off her figure. Her face mirrored Gene's almost identically, but of course, she was prettier, and her lips were fuller. Her hair was braided back into one long French braid, and the melanin in her soft brown skin made it seem like she hadn't aged a day.

"Thank you," Gene said to the guard after he uncuffed her. "You can leave now."

"I'll be right outside if you need me, sir." And with that, the guard exited.

"Gia, you look good," Gene said and motioned to the chair she was standing next to. "Sit."

"Why are you here?" Gia asked, looking into her brother's face. "These little secret meetings with me must cost a pretty penny."

Her voice was raspier than he remembered, but it still had that sweet undertone that used to get her whatever she wanted. Her soft face had hardened, which was to be expected. Prison had a way of bringing the ugly out in everyone, no matter how beautiful you were.

"When you have the governor on speed dial, you don't have to spend a dollar," he answered. "Now sit."

Gia looked from him to the chair as if contemplating if she should listen. In the end, she pulled the chair back and sat down. The two stared into each other's eyes for a moment before Gene smirked.

"You've been working out," he said.

"Not much to do in here. Might as well take care of my body so when I get out, I can enjoy the rest of my days."

"Hmm, good way to look at it," he said, and she scoffed.

"Let's cut the small talk. I'll ask you again. Why are you here?"

"I'm here because I have a question."

"Of course you do. What's your question, brother?"

"I need you to tell me everything you know about the man in this photo."

Gene pulled a small photograph out of the pocket of his suit and slid it across the table to her. Slowly she wrapped her small fingers around the corner of the picture and picked it up to get a closer look at it. A look of surprise crossed her face. It was quick, but Gene saw it.

"You didn't . . ." she finally breathed and looked up at him with a deep sadness in her eyes.

"I don't know what you're talking about," Gene replied.

Gia cleared her throat and placed the photo back on the table. She avoided eye contact with Gene for a few moments. It was almost as if he could see her thoughts going a mile a minute in front of him. She finally looked back at him and opened her mouth to speak.

"How is my son, Gene?" she said, pushing the picture back toward him. "I want to see him."

"No."

"You have kept him away from me for all these years! I have a right to see him."

"Not in the eyes of the law. And even if I told him you wanted to see him, he wouldn't come. Not after all those times you denied his visiting requests."

"Because you made me!" Gia said, banging her hands on the table. "You said you would kill him if he ever came to visit me."

"And that promise is still good enough to cash in on if you push me. You're a liability, Gia, and always have been. This prison is your heaven, because you should be dead. Never forget that."

"It's been years, Gene," Gia said with a plea in her eyes. "What could I possibly say to Andrew? I just want to see my son. I need to see my boy. You don't know what it's been like to be away from him for all this time. I can't imagine what he thinks about me . . . about his mother."

"And that's exactly why you'll do and say whatever you need to: so that you can clear that up. No."

"Gene, please."

"I asked you a question, and you haven't answered it yet."

"And I won't unless you agree to let me see my son."

Gene clenched his jaw. His sister had always had a stubbornness about her that seemed to get the best of him. They were two years apart, he being the older sibling, but she'd always been able to get what she wanted out of him some way or the other.

"A phone call. I will arrange for you to get a phone for this one purpose. But try to tell him anything and I will kill both of you myself."

"And I have your word?"

"As bond."

"Okay," Gia sighed happily. "Okay."

"Good, now tell me everything you know about Lucas Dubois."

Chapter 8

Never make a decision when you are upset,
sad, jealous, or in love.
—Mario Teguh

"Sss ah!" Belle whimpered and quickly put her finger to her lips.

She'd was sitting cross-legged on a king-sized bed in nothing but a milky silk robe and a burgundy lingerie set. For an hour she'd been counting and recounting the money she'd made the past two nights, when she got a paper cut. She instantly tasted blood and sucked until it went away. That was enough counting for the day. Her money was in a huge pile in front of her and amounted to just over $10,000. She couldn't believe that she had made that kind of money in two nights. It was easy money. All she had to do was smile and twerk something, and the money came pouring in. It was crazy.

That day the girls had decided to take a personal day before the last stop on the tour. They were in North Carolina, and that night the party they were doing would be for a group of basketball team owners. Belle was starting to get nervous because she knew that once they got to Miami, she would have to meet Gene for the first time. It put pressure on her to make the last nights of dancing count. That way, just in case he didn't want her to really be a part of Gene's Girls, she'd have enough money to start over somewhere.

"What am I thinking?" she said out loud, shaking her head at her thoughts.

Just in case he didn't want her to be a part of Gene's Girls? When did that ever become part of the plan? She'd originally just wanted to get enough money to go off on her own, but now for some reason, things were different. She'd grown attached to the other women, and the thought of never seeing Kidd again did something to the pit of her stomach. She regretted the way things ended between them the last time they spoke. But she knew that she would see him again soon. After all, he'd driven off in her car. She figured that she'd just get it back when they all got to Miami.

"You still counting that money, girl?" Russian poked her head into the room. Her long hair was pinned up with flexi rods, and her face was bare of all makeup. She was a beautiful woman naturally and surprisingly had full lips. Belle had been trying to figure out if they were real or if she had pulled a Kylie Jenner.

They were staying in a five-star hotel and had gotten a few suites to accommodate all of them. Belle was sharing one with Russian Roulette and Aria. Belle hadn't talked to them all morning, and she guessed that maybe she'd been quiet for a little too long.

"Yeah," Belle said and started neatly stacking the bills in thousands so that she could place rubber bands around them. "I just want to be sure my calculations are correct."

Russian invited herself inside the room and sat at the end of the bed, watching Belle. She too had on a robe that was tightly tied around her petite waist. Russian was quiet and didn't touch Belle's money. She just stared at her. Belle could feel herself growing warm because she knew Russian's eyes were on her. When she was done and the money was tucked back into the small duffle bag it had come out of, Belle focused her attention on Russian.

"You okay?"

"I could be asking you the same thing."

"Why is that? I'm fine."

"Are you sure?" Russian raised her eyebrow at Belle. "I've been seeing you popping those pills with Drip. I know they take the edge off, but they're too addictive, honey."

"What are you saying? That you think I can't handle myself? Why does everybody seem to think that I can't handle myself?"

"I'm just looking out for you, that's all," Russian said, ignoring the rise in Belle's tone. "Have you thought at all about what you're going to do?"

"Do about what?"

"I mean, when all of this is over," Russian said and waved her hands around for emphasis. "After tonight, there is only one more stop before we head home for a while. Are you going to stay in Miami?"

"I've been thinking about it," Belle told her. "In fact, Aria said that maybe I could stay and, you know, work for Gene permanently."

Russian's eyes widened at her words. "What do you mean, permanently?"

"As in become a permanent part of Gene's Girls. She even said that I would be able to go on tour all the time with you guys."

"Belle, I don't . . ." Russian closed her eyes briefly and shook her head. "I don't understand. Why would you choose this life?"

"The same reason you all did. The money."

"No. You don't understand. Once you choose this path, you will become a prisoner to it forever. You've already gotten enough money to start new somewhere."

"What do you mean, prisoner?"

Russian grabbed Belle's hands and held them tightly while staring into Belle's pupils. "I don't know what all you know, and the reason I didn't say anything is because I thought you'd be going your separate way soon. But this isn't a life you want. You've only seen the luxurious part of it. You haven't seen the ugly. And it gets ugly, Belle. And when it does, you can't go anywhere. The Bliss Lounge isn't what you think. It's—"

"That's enough, Russian."

Aria's voice caught them both off guard, and Russian Roulette dropped Belle's hands. The stern look Aria was giving her made her jump to her feet and hurry for the door. Before she was completely gone, she turned back to Belle and looked at her with sadness in her expression.

"One more thing," she said. "If you can't go out there and do what you need to do without a drug enhancement, then maybe this isn't the line of work for you. Get out while you can."

She sashayed away before Aria could say anything else to her, leaving Belle with a puzzled expression. It didn't go unnoticed by Aria, who sighed and sat down where Russian had just gotten up from.

"It's crazy that she can say anything to you about drugs when she pops pain pills like they're Tic Tacs," Aria said and tried to offer Belle a smile.

"What's the Bliss Lounge?" Belle asked, ignoring her.

"Why?"

"Because Russian was just about to tell me something about it before you cut her off. I know you kind of told me about it before, but you didn't go into much detail then."

Aria sighed again. "The Bliss Lounge is what Gene's Girls belong to. It's the place we come from."

"So it's like your headquarters or something?"

"Exactly. The Bliss Lounge is the main pleasure house. In order to be a part of such pleasure, one must purchase one of three memberships. The high-flying customers get treated to a stop in our tour."

"So it's like a brothel?"

Aria laughed out loud. "It's a gentlemen's club. The men don't merely come for pleasure. They come to fulfill their heart's desires. Sometimes that could be sex, other times it may be drugs, and sometimes it is to pour out their darkest secrets to a pretty face. The girls who work there—"

"Wait, there are other girls?"

"Of course there are other girls, silly. As big as the Bliss Lounge is, you're going to be thankful for that. Those girls don't get the same perks we do. They're paid a fixed salary and aren't allowed to take tips from the clients. We, on the other hand, get a salary and tips and get to live in our own homes."

"Get to?"

"What?"

"You said, 'get to.' Are the other girls not allowed to leave?"

"Yes, they can leave, but they have to come back."

"Or else what? Things will get ugly like Russian said?"

"Russian was just being dramatic. Don't listen to her. She's just trying to scare you because she knows her spot on Gene's Girls will be threatened. Technically we have one girl too many, and if Gene wants to keep you, he may kick one of them off. I mean, you've only been with us a short while and are already raking in the dough like a pro. It would be an easy decision."

"What did she mean when she said that if I chose this life, I'd become a prisoner to it forever? Is she talking about the other girls at the Bliss Lounge?"

"Those girls are on a contract, Belle. A contract they willfully signed. Understand that a lot of Gene's clients come to see and spend time with one specific girl. And if said girl breaks her contract by running off, it costs Gene money. Lots of money. Name one business owner who would be happy with that."

"I . . . I don't know any."

"Exactly."

"Then that means I'd have to sign too. A contract, I mean, in order to be officially a part of the Bliss Lounge?"

"We all sign contracts. It's like when you fill out the paperwork at any other job."

"Oh."

"Don't let the other girls scare you away," she said and stood up.

"They're just intimidated by my presence, right? What about you? If what you said is true, couldn't your spot be on the line too?" Belle asked, and Aria chuckled slightly as she walked to the door.

"Honey, I'm the head girl," she said, looking over her shoulder at Belle. "My spot is engraved in blood. Not even God could knock me from my spot. One thing Russian said was true, though."

"What's that?"

"You need to lay off those pills. A sober mind is a sharp mind, remember that. I'm about to go grab something to eat. Feel free to get dressed and join me if you want to."

She left, and when she was gone, Belle couldn't shake the uneasy feeling in the pit of her stomach.

"Not even God could knock me from my spot."

There was something about the way Aria said it that didn't sit right with Belle, but she put it to the back of her mind. Her stomach was growling, and it wasn't until then that she remembered that she hadn't put a single thing in her stomach. Before she got up, she grabbed the new cell phone she'd purchased since the other one she had was a part of the family plan she'd shared with her deceased family. She'd secretly gotten Kidd's number from Phil's phone the night before when he was busy raking Luscious's money up.

Hey. This is Belle. Lock me in. I'm sorry for the way things went the last time we talked.

She wanted to add more, but she didn't know what to say. She missed him and almost told him that, but she stopped herself. No point in saying it just in case he didn't text back. She hit send and proceeded to get dressed for the day. She had a lot to think about.

"Ahh, shit!" Ollie shouted as his shoulder jolted back. A casing from the gun he was shooting caught him in the eye by surprise, and he stopped shooting for a moment.

"I told you this is a place for big boys," Kidd joked and set his Glock 19 down on the table beside him in his lane.

"Shut yo' ass up, nigga. You can keep that boy shit. I'm a man."

"Yeah, the same man who used to cry when we didn't make curfew on time."

"Ay, man, chill with that," Ollie said and stepped out of his lane. "You know just like I do that my mama didn't play that shit."

Ollie had grown to be a tall, muscular man. He'd let his hair grow out, and he wore it in long locs that went down his back. That day he had them braided in four neat rows. He must have recently sat in a barber's chair, because his line was crispier than a plate of fried chicken. Same for his sideburns and the short beard on his chin. Like Kidd, Ollie liked to be well groomed. Appearance was everything to a king, and the last vibe either of them wanted to give off was that of a sucka. That day was a casual day for both of them. Cargo shirts and designer T-shirts hugged their muscles. Where Kidd had opted for Fendi, Ollie rocked Gucci all the way down to the socks.

"Whatever, man," Kidd said, checking his watch. "Where is this nigga at? It's been two hours already."

"All I know is that a nigga is hungrier than two BBWs," Ollie said, gripping his stomach. "And since Maria ain't here, I'm thinkin' we should go to that seafood spot by the beach."

"We can do that," Kidd said and pulled his phone out to make sure he hadn't missed a call due to the loud gunshots.

He didn't miss a call from Gene, but he did have a text message waiting to be opened from an unknown number. When he opened it and read the message, a smile he didn't even feel come on made its way to his cheeks.

Ollie gave him a knowing look and shook his head. "Who is she?"

"What you mean?" Kidd asked as he typed out a message: It's cool, shorty. You were doing your thing. I ain't mean to step on your toes. And don't worry about your car. She'll be here waiting for you when you get back. I'ma get it detailed for you, too.

"The only times I ever seen you smile like that is if money is involved or a bitch is. So which one is it?"

"Come on, man, let's go get this seafood you want so bad," Kidd said and patted Ollie's arm.

Before Ollie could interrogate him anymore, Kidd left the gun range and was making his way upstairs. He checked to make sure everything was good before they left the house and locked the door behind him. That day he'd opted to drive his own black-on-black G-Wagen instead of Belle's Camaro. It was more his style of car. He liked feeling the leather under his body and sitting up higher than the rest of traffic. It reminded him that he had made it out of the trenches despite all odds against him. Ollie offered to drive his BMW to the restaurant, but Kidd told him to hop in his whip. He hadn't been home for a whole month, and he wanted to push his own wheels around his city.

"Show off," Ollie said when he got into the passenger's seat. "I can't even lie, though. This bih kinda nice."

"Yeah, it's time for you to upgrade, my G," Kidd told him as he pulled out of the long, circular driveway. "That Beemer is nice and all, but you need a Ferrari or somethin'."

"Crazy you said that. I got one gettin' made for me as we speak."

"Oh, word?"

"Yeah. While you've been gone, Gene done had a young nigga puttin' in that work," Ollie said. "These last few jobs paid pretty good, and I figured I'd treat myself."

"That's what's up."

Kidd had gotten Gene to put Ollie on too once he saw the kind of money to be made. He didn't feel right balling out if his partner couldn't be right there with him. Together, the two were untouchable and the best hired shooting team. Sometimes the jobs they did were just security jobs for the girls, but most times they were more than that.

Gene had never completely given up the drug game. He just got smarter while in it. He had graduated from a king to an emperor, and he had the entire city on lock. Nothing came in or out of the city without him knowing it, and if he found out about any funny business, the problem would be dealt with. Kidd and Ollie were the ones who would deal with it.

It didn't take too long for them to get to the restaurant, and it felt as if Kidd had started starving on the way. Maybe it was because he was thinking about the shrimp and crab legs platter he was going to order, or maybe it was because he hadn't eaten all day. Whatever the case was, he was going to throw down. He parked near the entrance of the restaurant and got out. From where he stood, he could hear the soothing sound of waves smashing against the land, and he paused for a second. He turned his head to look at the beach in the distance and soaked in the beautiful scene.

"Damn, G, you've only been gone a month. You act like you ain't never seen the beach before."

"Some shit you just never get tired of. It makes you wonder how anyone could ever live anywhere but here."

"True that," Ollie agreed. "I can see myself travelling all over the world, but I can't see myself living anywhere but here."

"Come on," Kidd said after watching the water for a few more seconds. "Let's go get our eat on before we have to head back."

When they entered the restaurant, Crab Racks, Kidd took notice of a few other people eating there, but not many. Normally when he got food from there it was take-out, so he'd never taken the time to examine the place. It was decorated like the inside of a boat, with props like anchors and photos of fishermen hanging on the walls. It was nice, and Kidd loved seafood, so the smell of it was warming to his soul.

There was a short, petite woman standing at a podium waiting to seat them. She was pretty and wore her natural hair in two buns at the top of her head. The glasses on her nose suited her heart-shaped face, and she flashed a perfect smile their way. "Only two today?"

"Yeah," Ollie answered.

"Wow, that's surprising."

"What's that supposed to mean, Kiara?" Ollie asked after glancing at her name tag.

"I just assumed that men as handsome as the two of you surely had dates joining them."

"Nah, we don't do that datin' shit. Women are only good for one night around these parts," Ollie answered with a straight face, and Kiara's brow furrowed.

"Word?"

"Nah, I'm just fuckin' with you," Ollie told her with a grin. "But ay, can we get a booth though?"

"If you're single, you can get whatever you like," she said, batting her long eyelashes up at him before having the two men follow her to a booth. She waited for them to sit down across from each other at the booth before she handed them their menus. "Your server will be right over to help you, but if you need me, you know where to find me."

"Got it," Ollie said and watched her walk away. "Damn. Short girls be havin' the biggest booties. I'm getting her number before we leave. I'm tryin'a dive into that tonight."

"You're a whole fool, man," Kidd laughed. "What happened to that girl Shar you were into?"

"Man, that bih was crazy, dog," Ollie said and shook his head. "Shorty started leaving shit over my house, and at first I wasn't tripping. A pair of panties here, a shirt there. But then she cleared out a whole drawer for her shit and bought a toothbrush specifically for my house."

"What's wrong with that? I thought you were feelin' her."

"I was, but I wasn't tryin'a move her in with me or nothin' like that. She wasn't even my girl! I thought we were just havin' some fun, but she was tryin'a marry a nigga."

Kidd found himself laughing at the serious expression on Ollie's face. He couldn't say that his friend was a womanizer, but he could say that he was definitely a ladies' man. It was going to take a special woman to make Ollie settle down, and it was safe to say that she hadn't crossed his path yet.

"Eventually you gon' find that one who makes you want to leave the game behind you."

"Sike, nigga. Can't no bitch stop me from making all this paper."

"Yeah, yeah. You say that now. But watch, pretty soon one of these girls is gon' have you wide open."

"You're crazy."

At that moment, their server came over to take their orders. She was much older than Kiara, but she still had smooth golden brown skin and a youthful smile. There was a gray streak in her hair that she wore up in a pony-tail, giving her a look of wisdom. She had a beauty mark on her left cheek, and her eyes were the color of coffee.

"My name is Luella, and I'll be your server while you dine with us. How are you handsome gentlemen doing today?"

"We're just fine, ma'am, now that you've graced us with your presence," Ollie said with a smile.

"Oh, you better stop it," Luella told him with a grin. "You look like you're a hit with the younger ladies, but I've been around the block a few times. I know a too-smooth cat when I see one. What can I start you boys with to drink?"

"I'll take a Pepsi," Ollie told her.

"You can get me a Sprite," said Kidd.

"A Pepsi and a Sprite, got it," she said, jotting it down in her little notebook. She then glanced at the closed menus on the table in front of them. "Do you know what you want to eat, or do you need a few more moments to decide?"

"I'll take the crab legs platter," Kidd told her.

"And I'll have the Seafood Delight with extra shrimp, please, ma'am."

"Got it," she said with a smile. "I'll just take these menus out of your way and go . . ."

Her sudden pause in her sentence made Kidd look up at her, only to see that she was looking back at him too. She had a curious expression on her face, almost as if she suddenly recognized him.

"Is everything okay, ma'am?"

"Yes, yes. Everything is fine. You just remind me of somebody I know, that's all."

"He gets that all the time," Ollie joked. "If you think I'm a smooth cat with the ladies, Kidd here is a smooth criminal."

"Kidd. . . ." Luella repeated and let her voice trail off. She stared at him for a few more moments before he finally cleared his throat and snapped her out of her trance.

"Are you okay?" Kidd asked again.

"Yes. I'll go put these orders in for you right now."

She left without another word. When she was gone, Kidd raised his eyebrow at Ollie, who responded by shrugging his shoulders.

"If that bih poisons our food, I'm blamin' you," he said.

"Me? I've never seen that woman a day in my life, G. I don't know where she would know me from."

"Like I said, if we leave here and I drop dead somewhere, I expect you to pay for my funeral."

"Shit, if that's the case, I'ma be dead right along with you," Kidd retorted just as Luella brought them their drinks without giving either of them eye contact.

"Thank you," Ollie said to her, and she nodded.

"Anyways, nigga," Kidd said when she was gone and out of earshot, "tell me about these jobs that Gene has been sending you on while I've been away."

"The first couple were nothin' major," Ollie started after taking a gulp of his drink. "Just the standard 'collect what's owed' type of thing. I busted in on one motherfucka getting his dick sucked by three women, man. Some bad bitches, too. I told myself that after I whooped his ass and got Gene's paper, I gotta see what that feels like. I mean, I've had two bitches, but three? Man, I would go crazy. But anyway, at first it was just easy shit."

"And then?" Kidd asked. Ollie looked at him like he didn't want to say anything, so Kidd repeated himself. "And then?"

"Man, I didn't want to bring it up."

"Bring what up?"

"Gene called me to the house a few weeks ago and told me that he had a new job for me. He said it was a big job and since you were gone on tour that I would need some backup. I was just gon' grab a few of my own people, but he didn't want me to do that. He said that he wanted somebody he for sure knew was gon' get the job done. Said he had someone for me."

"Who?"

"Percy."

"Percy as in Perseus?" Kidd asked, and his interest piqued.

"Yeah, G. That Percy."

"What was the job?"

"This is where it gets strange. Gene told me that the job would be payin' three times as much as usual."

"Damn, that's a lot of bread. Why, though?" Kidd asked, and Ollie sighed.

"Because that time we wouldn't be recovering what Gene lost. We would be grabbing somethin' else."

"So what are you tryin'a say, he sent y'all on a robbery?" Kidd joked and gave a small laugh. When Ollie didn't laugh with him, his expression grew serious. "Are you sayin' that Gene sent you on a robbery?"

"Not robbery. A kidnapping, in Nebraska. It was supposed to be a quick grab and go, but shit turned ugly real fast. I was supposed to wait in the car just in case anything popped off outside while Percy and one of his men went in. But apparently ol' dude inside got the drop on him, and they had to kill everybody in the house."

"Wait." Kidd couldn't believe what he was hearing. "Did you say Nebraska?"

"Yeah."

"A family?"

"Yeah."

"Did you happen to get a name?"

"Nah, I didn't ask. And I'm wonderin' why you're askin' me so many questions right now."

"My bad," Kidd said, trying to play it off even though his thoughts were going haywire. "You know I like details."

"You're good," Ollie said.

Kidd's phone buzzed in his pocket, and he pulled it out. A part of him hoped it was Belle, and he was pleased to see that it was her. A part of him wished that he hadn't left. He read her message and sent a reply before placing the phone back in his pocket.

"That was her again, huh?"

"I don't know what you're talkin' about, man," Kidd said and drank his soda.

"Since when do we keep secrets? Now tell me, who is she?"

"You know, you're really too nosy for your own good," Kidd said, hoping that Ollie would drop it, but his friend just kept staring at him with a knowing look. "All right, nigga. Yes, it's a girl."

"What girl, though? Is she a jump off or is she wifey type?"

"I don't know yet. I'm still tryin' to figure all that out."

"Well, have you hit yet?"

"Nah, not yet. That's not what I'm on with her. I met her while I was on tour. She had gotten herself in a bad situation, and we brought her on the bus."

"On the bus? As in the Gene's Girls bus?"

"Yeah. She was in a little bit of a bind." Kidd paused himself before he said too much about Belle's situation. "She was in a bind, and Aria offered her a way to make a little cash.

"Those bitches turned her out, didn't they?" Ollie asked, and Kidd shrugged.

"I left before I had to see all that. I tried to tell her that she was too good for that life, but she wasn't tryin'a hear me."

"Well, you know if they did turn her out, she's off-limits to you now, don't you? Gene doesn't play that shit. He just blew Anthony's head off for dippin' his dick in Flare."

"Anthony?"

"He was a newer security dude. Either way, what I'm tryin'a say is we both know Gene doesn't like to mix business with pleasure. Nephew or not, I wouldn't do that shit if I were you, G. You know how he is about his girls. They're like his property."

"She's not his girl until she signs a contract."

"If she's already on that bus making money through his clients, she's already one of his girls," Ollie said.

Before Kidd could respond, Luella brought the two men their food. She set their dishes down in front of them. The aroma hit Kidd's nose and instantly made his mouth water. The awkwardness that Kidd had felt radiating from her was gone, and she spoke to them as if nothing strange had happened before.

"How does everything look for you?" she asked.

"Delicious. Y'all did hold the spit, right?" Ollie asked, and she raised her eyebrow in confusion.

"I'm sorry?"

"Nothin'. Everything looks good," Kidd said and shot Ollie a look, to which he responded with a grin of his own.

"Perfect. Y'all be sure to let me know if you need anything else, all right?"

"Thank you," Kidd said, and as quickly as she had come, she was gone again.

"Spit or no spit, I'm about to tear this shit down," Ollie claimed after saying his grace. "A nigga might even lick the plate!"

Kidd sat there watching him dig into his food like a wild animal. He was hungry, but Ollie's words were ringing in his mind like Christmas bells. He was right. Gene would consider Belle one of his girls off GP. He would look at all the money she'd made like a loan, as if it had come directly from his pockets. Kidd knew what happened to the girls once they became a part of Gene's world. It looked like sunshine and daisies, but the truth of the matter was that all of those shopping sprees came at a cost. A nightmarish one at that.

It was a fate he didn't want for Belle. She'd already suffered enough loss, and if she continued down that rabbit hole, it would cost her her soul. Not to mention that Gene was looking for her already. If the job Ollie spoke of was what Kidd thought, Belle being in the presence of Gene wasn't a good idea anyway. There was no telling what he would do to her. His plan was simple: intercept her before she met with Gene. If he had to pay his uncle out of his own pocket for Belle to keep her freedom, then so be it.

When they were done eating, they wasted no time paying the check and leaving. On his way out, Ollie made good on his word and got Kiara the hostess's number and told her he was going to hit her up later that night. Kidd hoped that they had killed enough time and Gene was back already. Sure enough, when they pulled back around the circular driveway, Gene's red Maybach was parked behind Ollie's car.

"What did he want you to slide over here for anyway?" Ollie asked, shutting the door of the G-Wagen behind him.

"Somethin' about Percy," Kidd answered, and the two of them went up the wide-set steps to the front door.

"Percy?"

"Yeah, he ain't really go into details over the phone," Kidd said, opening the front door. He went in first and looked around. "Unc!"

"Downstairs!" he heard his uncle's faraway voice shout.

They went down to the basement and found Gene sitting at his desk. As usual, he was dressed business savvy with a clean-cut head and face. When he saw the two boys enter, he told them both to sit down across from him.

"I expected to find you here when I returned," he said with a slightly raised eyebrow at Kidd.

"I didn't expect you to take all day," Kidd told him. "We got hungry, and since Maria's gone, we had to step out."

"Touché, nephew," Gene chuckled. "Anyhoo, straight to business then. Ollie, I'm glad you're here, being that you were with Percy the night that job went terribly wrong. I appreciate that you told me exactly what you saw and heard. When I entrusted Percy with assisting you, I thought the money being offered was what piqued his interest. That was foolish of me. I now know that Percy has set a personal vendetta against me. He sabotaged the job on purpose. The man I sent you in to grab wasn't supposed to die, no matter what. He knew that."

"Who was the man?" Kidd asked and held his breath.

"Lucas Dubois. He was the owner of a business that I was hoping to, say, do business with. I even allowed him to enjoy the amenities at the Bliss Lounge completely on me. He dabbled with a few house favorites and snorted the finest cocaine in Florida. He enjoyed himself thoroughly and didn't even know he was being recorded."

"Blackmail," Kidd said, stating the obvious. "You were trying to blackmail him into doing business with you? Why? Your client list is vast. You even have the governor on speed dial."

"Vast is still not big enough. How do large companies survive?"

"Expansion," Ollie answered.

"And what else?"

"Who you know?" Kidd guessed.

"Exactly. The Bliss Lounge is destined to be more than just a few locations. It should be worldwide. Lucas Dubois had the power to give me just that, and Percy may have tuned in to a conversation or two. So he knew what I was after. He hasn't gotten over that when the Bliss Lounge became hotter than even I imagined, I turned him away after he came back asking to be my security detail. He didn't understand how I could let kids—his words, not mine—run the show. Although I kept him in the loop whenever I needed extra hands, he never had a constant money flow again. Because of that, he wants to end me.

"See, the Bliss Lounge has slowed major product sales in the streets. I mean, why would the high flyers pay by the hit when they can pay a monthly fee and get as high as they want every day if they desire? Not to mention the pussy. It's a no-brainer."

"What do you want us to do?"

"I want you to take him and any other threat out. While I am expanding my business, I want a clear conscience. I don't want to be looking over my shoulder every ten seconds."

"But if Lucas Dubois is dead, how do you plan to expand? I'm assuming you were going to use his high-profile client list from his management company to do so."

Gene gave Kidd a strange look. "I never said what kind of company he ran," Gene said, furrowing his brow ever so slightly. "How did you know that?"

"I recognized the name as soon as you said it," Kidd said, thinking fast on his toes. "They broadcast his death and a few details about the deceased on the news when the bus was passing through the Midwest. And now, I just assumed his client list was what you were after all along."

"Always paying attention to detail," Gene said with a slow smile. "That's exactly why you're the best for the job. But yes, that was what I was after, and I'm still going to get it."

"How?"

"Percy thought by killing the entire family, I wouldn't get what I wanted. He was wrong. Lucas Dubois had a daughter."

"I thought they said she wasn't left anything because—"

"Because she isn't his birth child, I know. But there was something they left out. Something even she may not know. While he was high out of his mind at Bliss, he let something slip to one of my girls. He had an amended will in a safe inside of his house. In it, he stated that if anything should ever happen to him, his brother should take over his company. If ever his brother was not able to fulfill those duties, all ownership and responsibility should go to his children, Luca and Belle Dubois. So now all I have to do is kill the brother and find the daughter."

"Why not just get the brother to give you what you want?" Kidd asked.

"Because a man given power like that won't let it go so easily. I'd rather save myself the time. But Belle? That will be too easy."

Gene grinned like the Cheshire Cat, and Kidd didn't like the look in his eye. He held his tongue, however, and tried not to let his face show any emotion.

"First, I need you to kill Percy and everyone loyal to him. Next, I'll be sending you to Nebraska to handle the brother. You will be compensated nicely for your duties, of course. And, Kidd, you can take that month off you want so badly. Any objections?"

"Shit, not from me, boss," Ollie said. "You know I'm always down to make some extra coin. And I never liked that nigga Percy anyway."

Chapter 9

*I do quite naughty things now. I do
like to be a bit sexy.*
                    —Kylie Minogue

*Look, my bitches all bad, my niggas all real
I ride on his dick, in some big tall heels*
Cardi B's voice filled the entire house up as Gene's
Girls once again did their thing. That night, the clients
were all millionaires, and the money started falling the
moment they walked through the door. Russian's words
stuck with Belle, so that night when Drip offered her
a pill to pop, she refused it. Russian was right. If she
couldn't get the job done sober, then there was no point
in her being there. Surprisingly, when it was her turn to
take over the floor, her nerves weren't bad at all. She was
still getting used to the pole, but she knew enough tricks
to make the crowd go crazy.
*I got bands in the coupe
Bustin' out the roof
I got bands in the coupe
Touch me, I'll shoot*
Belle twerked to the beat of the song, and she could
feel her ass going in a circle. She'd gotten used to the feel
of the money falling over her near-naked body, but that
didn't make her love it any less.

When the song was over, Phil raked all of her money to the side in the living room of the mansion. All of the girls had their own piles, and so far, hers was the biggest. As she walked in her five-inch heels to the kitchen, she noticed one of the guys whispering to Aria and pointing at and looking at her. He was a handsome white man, probably in his mid-30s. He was muscular and had brunette hair and sandy brown eyes. He was clean-shaven with a perfect smile. Belle paid no mind to them. He was probably asking Aria to get a private dance with her, which she didn't mind doing. She just needed to quench her thirst first. All of that dancing had made her hotter than ever.

The kitchen in the mansion was just as big and lavish as the living room. There was a wide marble island close to the sink that Belle ran her fingers over as she passed. She opened every white wooden cabinet door until she found a glass. She took it to the sink and filled it with cold water before pressing it to her pink lips and taking a big gulp.

"Hey," Aria's voice came from behind her.

Belle turned around and realized that Aria must have followed her to the kitchen. That night Aria was wearing a sultry see-through black teddy with the matching sheer robe. Her ankle-strapped stiletto heels were at least six inches, and they made her plump bottom sit up perfectly. On her head was a long black wig with a middle part. The smoky eye shadow gave her a darker look than what Belle was used to seeing on her, but still, she was beautiful.

"Hey."

"You did your thing on that pole! I see you've been practicing those moves the girls have been teaching you."

"Yeah," Belle said with a smirk. "It feels like I've been doing this shit forever. It hasn't even been three weeks."

"You're a natural. Got that money rolling in. Pretty soon you're going to need two duffle bags to store it in," Aria said, moving a piece of Belle's hair from her face. "You see that guy I was talking to?"

"The good-looking one?"

"Yes, him."

"What about him? He want a dance or something?"

"Yes, he wants a private dance in one of the bedrooms."

Her words made Belle stop sipping the water in her hands and set the glass down. She gave Aria a puzzled look. "You mean away from the other girls?"

"That's what private dance means, doesn't it?"

"I guess, but . . ."

"But?"

"I haven't done that before. I mean, I've given solo dances, but always in the main party area."

"Then what's the big deal? That cracker is probably planning on dropping major bread on you."

"Is . . . is that all I have to do?"

"Dance?"

"Yeah. I'm not really with any of that extra shit."

"You talking about fucking him?"

Belle didn't answer. She just picked her glass back up and downed the water to the last drop. She suddenly felt the jitters that she'd been doing a good job keeping at bay. They crept up on her like a robber in a home invasion until soon they took over her body.

"Relax, bitch," Aria told her. "You don't have to do anything that you don't want to do. All right?"

"All right."

"Now if your thirst is quenched, follow me. He's already in the bedroom waiting for you."

"Okay," Belle said and took a few wobbly steps after her.

She didn't know why she felt like her legs were working ten times harder at holding up her weight. It was almost as if she were next up to perform and suddenly caught a bad case of stage fright. Either way, she felt intimidated. More intimidated than she felt the first night she danced, but she remembered that was because Drip helped her out with that.

Belle took a big breath when Aria led her upstairs and to the end of a long hallway. A bedroom door was open, and Belle assumed by its large size that it was the master. Sure enough, upon entering, Belle saw the same guy Aria was talking to sitting on a king-sized bed with a stack of money beside him. When he saw her come in, she instantly saw the look of pure lust pass over his face.

"Beauty, this is Billie. Have fun," Aria said and winked at Belle. Before she left, she leaned and whispered in Belle's ear, "Phil will be right outside the door."

Aria left faster than Belle would have liked, but why wouldn't she? Belle had been rocking the house the last few parties. She had long since tossed her training wheels aside. She glanced over her shoulder and watched the bedroom door close behind her before she turned back to Billie. He probably didn't even notice her discomfort or that she was rubbing her hands up and down her thighs out of nervousness. No. His eyes were too busy taking their time on her body.

They started at her full, pouty lips and traveled down to her neck. Soon they found their way to her plump breasts and the way they sat in the plum-colored push-up brassiere she'd decided on for the night. The thong she wore matched and had gotten swallowed between the cheeks of her voluptuous butt. When his chilling blue eyes were done there, they traveled to her flat stomach before landing on her thick thighs. He licked his lips, probably wondering how they felt. At last, when they reached her crotch, she couldn't stand it any longer. She cleared her throat.

"Excuse me for a second please," she said and started toward the bathroom in the bedroom.

"No, take your time," he said with a smile. "I won't be going anywhere."

She tried to give him a seductive smile before she rushed to the bathroom. As soon as she flicked on the light, she shut the door behind her and locked it. Pressing her back to it, she slid to the floor with her eyes closed. Placing a hand on her chest, she could literally feel how hard her chest was pounding. Why this? Why now? Every emotion that she'd been suppressing was coming up and staying firm in her mind. Her grief, her sadness, and most of all, her anger. She was all alone, and the people around her were truly strangers. Her father's face came to mind, and she clenched her eyes shut, begging him to go away. She could see the disappointment in Lucas Dubois's eyes looking at her cowered down in the bathroom.

A stripper. That's what she had become. Exotic dancer was just the less derogatory name for it. She had become a woman who used the allure of pussy to get a dollar.

Belle stood up and walked slowly toward the mirror. She saw herself all made up like a porcelain doll. Every wand curl in her hair was still perfectly in place. There were some beads of sweat across her forehead due to her nerves. All she wanted to do was walk out of that bathroom and leave the house altogether, but she didn't know how far she'd get. She wondered if anyone would try to stop her. But where would she go? She had no home to go to. Her uncle hadn't even tried to get in contact with her once since she'd been gone. All she had was herself, and that was what she would have to use to survive.

Belle pushed her father's disappointed expression out of her mind and reached in her bra. She had been confident that she wouldn't need the pill, but she brought it anyway. As a "just in case" precaution. There were little paper Dixie cups next to the sink, and she filled one of them with cold water. She stared at the pill in the palm of her hand for a few moments, debating what her next move would be.

"Everything all right in there?" Billie called to her.

"Yes," she replied and quickly popped the pill and drank the small shot of water. "I'll be right out."

She counted to sixty three times before she opened the bathroom door. There were two things that were different about the room. First, it was darker, and the lamps had red bulbs shining in them. Second, Billie had made himself extremely comfortable. No longer was he wearing his suit jacket and crisp slacks. Instead, he was in a pair of Versace briefs and a T-shirt.

"I hope you don't mind that I got a little comfy," he said, standing from the bed when she came out. "I rarely wear clothes in my bedroom."

"This . . . this is your bedroom?"

"It is. Are you not impressed?" he joked and looked around the room. "I thought the lion rug upon entering and deep red drapes were definite lady killers."

"Oh, they are," Belle hurried to say, not wanting to offend him. "Nice, I mean."

"I'm just fooling," he said and flashed her his perfect smile. "I have to say, your name is more than fitting. You are by far one of the most beautiful women I have ever seen, and that says something. As a successful business owner, I've had my share of pretty women, but you have them all beat."

Belle's pill had started to kick in, and she felt it coming over her body. It could be compared to the carefree sensation one might feel after those four straight shots of Hennessy. Her skin tingled from her face to her toes, and she didn't understand why she had ever tried to give up the feeling. That time when she rubbed her thighs, it wasn't because her nerves were bad. No. It was because she was enjoying how smooth they were, and she knew they were going to get her the big bucks that night.

"Are you going to stay so far away from me?" he asked.

"I didn't come in here to be away from you," she answered. Even her voice had changed. Gone was the timid tone of Belle, and welcomed was the sexiness of Beauty. She batted her long eyelashes at him and saw him with a different set of eyes. She wasn't intimidated by him any longer as she assessed him. The bedroom, his bedroom, screamed, "King," and she could tell that he treated and even viewed himself as royalty. She could also tell, based on the small bulge in his briefs, that he was definitely overcompensating. *Line 'em up, then knock 'em down.*

"Why did you choose me out of all the girls for a dance?" Belle asked as she walked slowly to him.

"I already told you. You're beautiful," he answered.

"Is that the only reason?" she asked when she was so close to him that her breasts were almost touching him.

Her nearness caused Billie's breathing to turn shallow as he looked down at her. She matched his stare with an intense one of her own. She didn't smell a lick of alcohol on his breath, so he might not have been unknowingly generous to her. With him, she might have to do a little more than just smile and shake her thighs in his face. She would have to fuck his mind up.

"No," he said in a low tone.

"Is it because of my fat ass?" she asked, turning around so he could get a better view.

She bent down low and came back up slowly, looking over her shoulder. Pressing her bare butt on his crotch, she forcefully nudged him so that he fell back onto the bed. Seeing his stuck expression, she giggled. There was no music, but Belle didn't need any. She put her hands on her knees and sensually rotated her back in a circle. The movement caused her thighs to shake like an earthquake as her bottom went up and down.

"Yes," he answered with his eyes transfixed on her, and she giggled again.

"Or maybe it's my luscious titties," she said, standing up and turning to face him.

She allowed him to mush his face in her chest as she shimmied. When she felt his tongue between her breasts, she drew back and wagged a finger at him.

"Ah ah, you naughty boy you," she said with a wink.

"I am a naughty boy," he said and licked his lips. "Come show me how you punish us bad boys."

"I can do that," she said and walked over to his dresser where he had a wireless speaker.

He had an MP3 player next to it, and Belle quickly found the song she wanted to dance to: August Alsina's "Like You Love Me." His voice was so smooth to her, and it was easy for her to move her body to it once she heard his first note. By then, Belle was so high that she barely felt her feet moving. She danced in front of Billie, on him, and even on the bed around him. By the time the song was over, he had already thrown the majority of the stack of twenties beside him. On August's last note, Billie just grabbed the remainder of the stack of money and handed it to her.

"Please just stay for a few more moments," he begged. "I don't deserve to be inside of a woman as stunning you. But please, let me relieve myself in your presence, and you can have all of my money."

He didn't wait for Belle to give him the okay before he pulled his briefs down. His penis was bigger than what Belle had thought, and he grabbed a bottle of oil from his nightstand beside his bed. He put a little in his hand before wrapping it around his erection. It wasn't the first time that Belle had seen a white man's manhood, but that didn't make it any more appealing. It was paler than the rest of his body, and the head of it reddened with each stroke from his hand.

Belle stood in front of him, not knowing what to do, but the money in her hand felt so good, and she thought it was best to stand there although the song was over. She couldn't lie, seeing him pleasuring himself to just the sight of her turned her on. It also reminded her that it had been such a long time since the last time she herself was intimate. His eyes explored her body as he jacked himself off, and she slowly began to touch herself. It wasn't until her hand fell between her legs that she realized just how turned on she was.

The moment her fingers touched her swollen clit, her body jolted with electricity. Moving her panties to the side, Belle slid her fingers between her plump second set of lips and felt how moist she'd become. Her pussy was hungry to feel an orgasm, and once she started circling her clit with her middle finger, she couldn't stop.

"Mmmm," she moaned, feeling her legs give out under her.

She fell gently to the ground, lay on her back, and spread her legs. She put the stack of money in her hand beside her face, so close that she could feel it on her cheek. Billie had the perfect view of her pretty shaved pussy, and she could see him stroking his dick and rubbing his own ball sack. The carpet was so soft underneath her, and she pulled her bra down to expose her chocolate nipples.

"Yeah, rub that pussy, baby," Billie moaned. "Imagine it's my tongue sucking and licking all over that fat clit. Imagine my big white cock stroking that pretty pussy. That pretty shaved pussy, Beauty."

There was something about the low growl in his undertone that made her clit jump. Her own juices flowed all over her fingers, making her entire hand sticky. She moved her hips in a circular motion as she pleased herself. Using her free hand, she began rubbing her breasts softly and pinching them every so often. The sensation was so blissful that her back arched. She felt her climax getting closer and closer until—

"Ahhhh!" Billie shouted and emptied his ball sack into the air. "Fuck! You sexy-ass bitch!"

His semen shot up and hit the carpet right beside Belle's thigh, but she didn't care because she came at the same time. Her back arched in a way that made her full breasts jiggle, and she let her sticky nectar drip onto the carpet under her. The spot beneath her bottom was wet, but she didn't move until she caught her breath.

"That was beautiful," Billie said when Belle fixed her bra.

He pulled his briefs up and helped her off the ground. Before she got up, however, she placed a stack of money in her garter and left the rest strewn over the floor for Phil to come and get. The intensity she experienced from the orgasm made her legs a little shaky, but she was able to stand on them. Belle fixed her bra and blew Billie a kiss.

"I hope you enjoyed yourself," Belle told him, going for the door.

"Lady Passion told me you would be worth that whole five thousand, and she was right. Maybe I'll see you the next time I'm in Miami?" Billie asked in a hopeful voice.

"Maybe," Belle answered and left the room.

When Belle opened the door, sure enough, Phil was standing outside with his arms folded. When she passed, he went in the room to collect her money. All she wanted to do was get downstairs to where the other girls were so that she could have a drink before her next dance, and that time she didn't want any water. As she made her way down the hallway, she heard a commotion coming from one of the rooms she passed. It didn't sound like the usual fun and giggles that she had grown accustomed to. It sounded like someone was having a full-on tussle. Belle pressed her ear to the door so that she could hear exactly what was going on. There was a crash that was followed by what sounded like a smack.

"So this is why you've been so tired after every party, Cream?"

Belle recognized the voice instantly. It was Aria. She'd never heard her sound so angry before.

"Lady Passion, I'm sorry. I won't do it anymore. Please don't—"

Slap!

"Bitch, don't beg now!" Slap! "You've been stealing coke for months now!" Slap! "I knew something was off when I bagged the shit for the parties. And now I know why."

"Please, Lady Passion. I just needed it to cope."

"Cope with what?"

"This life! I was supposed to be done by now, but Gene won't let me leave," Cream said through her hard sobs. "I just want to go home. I just want to see my family."

"Supposed to be? You signed a contract, Cream. What did you expect? That whenever you were ready to go, you'd be able to walk out the door? You signed your life away for ten years, and that's what you're going to give. The only way you'll get out of it is if I catch you stealing again because I'll kill you. Do you understand?"

Silence.

"I said, do you understand?"

"You're almost worse than him," Cream said in a weak voice. "You can treat us however you want because you don't value us. And you don't value us because you don't value yourself."

"Oh, how cute. Bitch, you don't know anything about me. But I can show you better than I can tell you," Aria said and began beating Cream relentlessly.

Belle heard it through the door. She could almost feel every thud she heard as Aria landed blow after blow to Cream. She heard Cream screaming out in agony, but nobody could hear her but Belle. Whenever Belle thought Aria would stop, she just kept going. She wanted to open the door and help. Tell Aria to stop, something. But she was frozen in terror. It was her first time experiencing Aria as Lady Passion, and Belle wanted no part of it.

"Now go clean your face and go back out to the bus. I don't need your ugly ass fucking up the rest of my girls' money tonight. Let this be a lesson to you, especially if you ever want to see your family again. You'll be of no use to them if you come back empty-handed and without a dime to your name."

Belle heard feet coming to the door, and she hurried down the hallway and stairs. She didn't look back, and she tried to fix her face like she hadn't witnessed what had just happened to Cream. There was a punch bowl on a table in the living room filled with a spiked red drink. She poured some in a cup and downed it like water. She was still high, and her heart was pounding ferociously in her chest. What had she gotten herself into? Aria had seemed so sweet and nice, but now Belle was looking at her in a whole new light.

When Cream finally made her way down the stairs, she kept her head down. Belle glanced over her shoulder at her, and her stomach instantly felt like the drink she'd just swallowed was filled with needles. Cream's face was swollen, her lip was busted, and there were shadows of streaming mascara like she'd tried to wash her face, but not all of the makeup would come off. The once-neat bun on top of her head was wild, and she walked with a limp.

"Cream, I . . ." Belle started but stopped. She didn't know what to say. What could she say?

Cream walked past her, and it was like nobody else even noticed. Belle looked around the party and saw Dynasty taking shots from Luscious's belly button while twerking. Drip and Blessing were doing a dual number on the pole, and all of the men were in a daze. Belle had just refilled her glass when she heard somebody come up behind her.

"You all right?"

Belle turned around to see Russian Roulette standing there with a cup in her own hand. The black lace thong teddy she wore literally only covered her nipples and her sides. The jet-black material and the ruby red lipstick on her lips made her white skin seem even paler.

"Yeah," Belle lied at first and then shook her head. "No. I just . . . I just . . ."

"You just what, sugar?"

"Cream . . ." Belle shook her head, trying to make sense of it. "Aria was mad at her and just beat her. She beat her like a dog, and I heard the whole thing. She wouldn't stop. I was outside the door, and I should have tried to help, but I didn't. I couldn't. I've never seen Aria like that."

"Aria?" Russian Roulette scoffed. "Oh, that's right, she's still Aria to you. She was just Aria to me too once. But she turned into Lady Passion the moment I signed my contract."

"What?"

"I told you you're not fit for this life, sugar," Russian said. "You'd do best to just take the money you've made and go. What happened to Cream is what happens to anyone who does anything that they don't like."

"Aria said that she was stealing."

"She might have been. But you saw just like I did the way she looked when she walked out of here. Nobody deserves that. Especially when you've given up your whole life for this. We're prisoners. They watch everything we do. And Lady Passion is so loyal to Gene that it doesn't matter what kind of friendship you think the two of you have formed. She'll do you the way she did

Cream in a heartbeat. You're a good girl, Belle. Smart, sweet, compassionate. But Lady Passion only sees your face and your body. I guarantee you that she's already put a price on you just because you're so beautiful. They use the money and lavish life to lure us in, and once we're in, we're stuck like mice in traps. Did you pick your own name?"

"No," Belle said. "She did, that first night."

"Exactly."

"If it's so bad, then why are you still here?"

"My contract is up after this tour. I gave Gene five years of my life and stacked up enough paper to live good for a long time. I won't be here to see what you decide, but whatever it is, just do me a favor and be careful, okay?" Russian turned away from Belle and went back to a group of men huddled around the pole. "Who's ready to see all this white ass on the pole? I'm only accepting fifties and hundreds tonight, boys! No cheapskates will be tolerated."

Her words replayed in Belle's mind as she downed two more cups of punch. She thought about Aria and how quick she was to allow Belle on the tour bus with them all. Belle had been so distraught and down on her luck that she just thought Aria was being a kindhearted person. What if it was deeper than that? Belle reflected on it when she saw Aria talking to Billie.

"Lady Passion told me you would be worth that whole five thousand."

Had Aria placed a price on her without Belle knowing about it? Belle felt woozy, and she didn't know if it was because of the alcohol or because of everything else hitting her at once. She caught herself on the table and tried to steady her body. The room around her was spinning, and she focused on one spot on the tan carpet until everything stopped going in a circle.

Finally, she looked up and almost jumped. Standing at the top of the stairs was Aria, and she was looking directly at Belle. The smile on her lips was the last thing Belle saw before she threw up everything in her stomach.

Chapter 10

Success breeds complacency. Complacency breeds failure. Only the paranoid survive.
—Andy Grove

Kidd lay on his back in his circular king-sized bed, staring at the ceiling. His thoughts had caused him to come out of his sleep earlier than he would have liked to. The digital clock on his nightstand said that it was four in the morning, and by the darkness outside, he knew it was telling the truth.

"Mmm," a soft moan came from beside him.

He turned his head to the right and saw that one of his guests for the night had stirred in her sleep. She was a petite Filipino beauty named Willow whose long, silky hair went all the way down to her tight butt. He usually liked his women a little thicker, but the things she did with her mouth in his private VIP section the night before solidified her spot in his bed.

"Can't sleep?" a voice said from his left.

Kidd turned his head to his other side and saw a smooth chocolate face staring up into his. Diamond was pretty and wore long extensions in her hair. He could see her pear-shaped silhouette underneath the sheets. Both women beside him were naked, and he liked how their warm skin felt up against his. He'd had a wild night, and everything the three of them had done came rushing back to him. Instantly he got a hard-on, and his thick eight-inch erection pointed straight up under the white sheet.

"Oh, I get it," Diamond said and kissed his bottom lip with her full juicy ones. "You didn't get enough, and you want more, right?"

Her hand trailed down his upper body until it found what it was searching for. Her firm grip on his dick made Kidd suck in a breath through his teeth. She used her thumb to caress the head while her lips and tongue worked on his neck.

"Mmm," he moaned and went to wake Willow up so she could join the party.

Diamond stopped him and shook her head. "Let that bitch sleep," she whispered. "I want this dick all to my-self. I was pissed I had to keep sharing. It's so big, I want you to tear me up. Okay?"

"Okay," Kidd told her and grabbed her roughly by the back of her head. "If you want it all to yourself, I need you to suck it better than she did."

He pushed her head under the covers until he felt her lips wrap around his shaft. She slurped, spit on, and sucked him like a pro. His toes curled a few times, and watching her head bob up and down while she topped him under the sheets sent tingles up his spine. He placed both hands on her head and thrust up, forcing his dick to go as far down her throat as it would go. She choked and came up, gasping for air, but he only let her get a few breaths in before he did it again. And again.

It wasn't that he didn't respect women. He did. But Diamond wasn't his wife or girlfriend. He didn't care about pleasing her. She was his human masturbation device, and since she had chosen to stay the night, she would have to earn her keep.

Kidd reached under the sheets and pulled her up by her shoulders until she straddled him. He grabbed a condom from his nightstand and put it on before allowing Diamond to slide down on him. She must have turned herself on while she was sucking him off, because she was wetter than a lake. While her pussy swallowed him whole as she bounced up and down, Kidd buried his head in her breasts. His mouth shifted from nipple to nipple as he sucked, bit, and licked them like chocolate drops. His hands squeezed her round bottom and made her come down on him harder with each stroke.

"Damn, daddy," she moaned and shook her head. "It's so big. I can't take it."

"Nah, this is what you wanted, remember?" Kidd said and flipped her over so that he was on top. He never stopped stroking her pussy, and now he was in charge. "This is what you wanted, right?"

"Yes, baby! Yes!"

He wrapped his hand around her neck and applied a little bit of pressure while he fucked her harder than he intended to. It felt too good for him to stop, and her body was so soft under his. He circled his hips with each thrust to ensure that every sensation in her love tunnel felt him, and he didn't pay her any mind when she began screaming out that she was cumming. He wasn't fucking her for that.

"Shut up and take this dick," he told her, pressing his forehead on hers. "Open your legs wider."

Diamond's bottom lip quivered, and she batted her long eyelashes up at him. She did as he asked, and Kidd placed his hands behind her knees so that he could keep them wide open. He had beads of sweat dripping down his forehead, and the room had suddenly gotten hotter, but he ignored it all. His focus was on Diamond's thick body beneath him and his dick sliding in and out of her. He was turning himself on by the second and knew that soon he was going to explo—

"Ahhhh!" he shouted and thrust himself as far into her as he could.

He was sure that he had destroyed her cervix, and he didn't care one bit. His manhood pulsated in her as every last drop of semen poured out of his ball sack and into the condom. Kidd fell on top of her and buried his face in her neck until his climax washed over him. When finally it had passed, he kissed her neck and sucked her nipples one last time before pulling out of her and falling on his back. His chest heaved up and down as he tried to catch his breath. His dick had gone limp inside of the condom, and he looked over at Willow and saw that she was still sleeping.

"That bitch was rolling when we got here," Diamond said, cuddling up to him. "She's gon' be passed out for a while."

"Hopefully she's awake by eight, because that's when y'all gotta go."

"Damn," Diamond said, nibbling on his ear. "That's in a few hours. She gon' just miss out. Can I have it again, daddy?"

"Again?" Kidd asked astonished and looked down into her hungry face.

"Yes. I have a flight to catch later to go back home. Ain't no nigga in Mississippi who can fuck me like that. I want you to bend me over and put it in my ass."

Kidd looked down at her, and in the dimness of the room, he could have sworn he saw Belle's face on her. He could have promised that it was Belle's face staring at him with eyes begging for him to fuck her. To please her. To give her what she needed. Before he could even blink again, he had another hard-on.

"Hand me a condom."

"Long night?"

Kidd didn't even hear his partner talking to him. His head was leaning against the window of Ollie's BMW, and he was lost in his own head. Not to mention that his body was a little sore from all the sexing he and Diamond did. They'd gone on for hours until the sun came up, and before he knew it, it was time for the girls to leave and for him to start his day. Going on five hours of sleep wasn't anything new to him as he moved around scoping the city out with Ollie. The day passed by quickly, and soon, the girls were just a distant memory.

"Earth to Kidd. Ay, nigga?"

"My bad, Ollie. What did you say?"

"I said you must have had a long night. You took them bitches back to your crib after the club was over last night?"

"Yeah," Kidd said with a small smirk at his friend. "I figured I'd start my break a little early."

"Fuck that, your break starts after we handle this business," Ollie said, whipping the BMW with one hand into their old neighborhood. "But with that being said, those were two bad bitches. You're lucky that you got to 'em first."

Kidd grinned and pulled a black hood over his head when he felt the car slow down. Since Gene wasn't in the field any longer, it was up to Kidd and Ollie to figure out exactly where Percy was going to be. He was a slippery snake, and whenever they thought they had it figured out, they were wrong. It took them almost two days to figure out that Percy liked to hang out in a run-down house not too far from where they grew up. They watched the ins and outs of the small white house to see what they were up against, and sure enough, Percy always kept a mini army around him. No matter. Kidd was going to hit his mark.

"Load up," he said to Ollie.

Kidd tucked two pistols on both of his hips and held an AK-47 in his hands. Ollie did the same. In order to infiltrate the house, they would have to hit them hard, especially with not knowing who all was in there. Kidd looked over to see Ollie tucking an explosive in his pocket, and he raised his eyebrow.

"What?" Ollie asked. "This shit will take out most of them no question. Then you can get in and do what you gotta do."

"Word. Let's go. We gotta get in and get out before them crackas show up and air this bitch out."

The two men hopped out of the vehicle and trucked it the rest of the way to the house. They were cloaked by the night sky but still stayed as low as they could. Kidd stayed back slightly, and Ollie handed him his assault rifle. Kidd watched from a bush as his friend approached the house first. Standing outside like watchdogs were four of Percy's men wearing normal street clothes and laced in jewelry. They held beers in their hands and were in the middle of a heated debate.

"Halle Berry is the baddest female on the earth. Nigga, what is you talkin' 'bout?" said one of them with dreads longer than Ollie's.

"Man, that old bitch? Her pussy probably don't even get wet no more. Probably all powder down there. We all know Meagan Good holds the title for the baddest bitch in the universe!"

"Hell nah! She all saved and shit now. She probably forgot where the dick go. Ay, man, who the fuck is you?"

Their conversation ceased the moment Ollie appeared in front of them. Their eyes instantly went to his all-black attire, looking him up and down. The scowls on their face showed that they weren't very welcoming, and the two in the back had their pistols drawn within seconds.

"Whoa, whoa," Ollie said to them with his hands up. "There ain't no need for all that."

"What you want, nigga? Coming over here dressed like the grim reaper and shit. You must be stupid or somethin'."

"Nah, not stupid. Is Percy here?"

"Who's askin'?" the one with the dreads spoke and spit toward Ollie's black retro 13s.

"Nobody you need to know."

"Ay, I know this nigga," one of the men in the back said. The high-top afro on his head had been dyed completely blond, and he had a face that resembled a gorilla's. He lowered his weapon and stepped up past the other men to look Ollie up and down. "This is the fool who came with boss and me on that last hit."

"The one when y'all bodied that family?" dread head asked.

"Hell yeah. This chump stayed in the car like a good boy."

"Yeah, 'cause if I had come in, that shit wouldn't have gone down like that," Ollie said. "Word on the street is that your boss only accepted that job to fuck up what my boss has goin' on. And I'm here to see if that word is true. He in the basement?"

"No basement, nigga."

"Aw, that's straight then. He's in the front room then. Go tell that nigga I'm here."

"And if I don't?" the blond-haired man said, getting in Ollie's face.

"I guess you're about to see," Ollie said and put his hands behind his back just as Kidd started spraying.

The men didn't even have time to shoot, and even if they had, they wouldn't have known where to aim. They didn't stand a chance against Kidd's aim. The man standing in front of Ollie got his head snapped to the side when a bullet caught him in the temple, and the others dropped like flies behind him. The door to the house flew open, and Kidd took care of anyone who thought they were coming through the door. Ollie used that as his opportunity to pull the pin on the military-issued grenade and throw it through the door. He jumped to the side to take cover, and when it exploded, the entire neighborhood shook. The glass windows on the house had gotten blown out from the blast, and some of the wood was on fire.

"Here," Kidd said, handing Ollie his gun back and walking inside the house.

The smoke inside was still clearing, but from the looks of it, everyone was down. In the far back of what used to be the living room was a man Kidd instantly recognized. Percy was still alive and trying to crawl away. His face was covered in debris, and he was bleeding from the many cuts now on his body.

Bang!

Kidd whipped around when he heard the gunshot behind him and aimed his gun, but he saw that it was only Ollie. His assault rifle was hanging in his hand, but he had a pistol out pointing at one of the bodies.

"He wasn't dead. I saw him move," Ollie said, shrugging sheepishly. "Go do what we came to do, G. I'll be right back."

Kidd nodded and walked over to where Percy was. When he got close enough, Percy spit a huge glob of blood his way.

"Fuck you," he said, staring up with hatred in his eyes.

"I bet you never would have thought that the last face you'd see would be mine," Kidd said, aiming his gun at Percy. "Any last words?"

Percy then surprised Kidd by laughing. It was a deep, hearty laugh, mixed with a few coughs, but still, he must have thought something was hysterical.

"What's funny?"

"You."

"I don't see how that can be possible. From where I'm standing, I should be the amused one. I have a gun aimed at Perseus, the powerful demigod."

"You don't get it," Percy said before going into a fit of coughs. "After all these years, you still don't see shit for what it is. Gene has you wrapped so tight around the same finger he uses to fuck everybody else around him in the ass."

"What are you talkin' about?"

"I'm talking about the man you work for. Your uncle. You don't know him. Not like I do. He ain't worth shit."

"This coming from the nigga who sabotaged him."

"Touché, but I have my reasons to go against him. He blocked a lot of money for me, so I was just returning the favor. But you do know that's not the real reason he sent you here to kill me, don't you? If that's the case, he could have easily done so after he paid me for the job. No. He sent you here because I found out the truth that night he gave me my money."

"The truth?"

"Gene is a monster. I thought I was bad, but he's the green gunk on the bottom of worst's shoe. He'll take out anybody who gets in his way. Even you."

"My uncle wouldn't hurt me."

"Oh yeah? How about you ask your mother?" Percy said and laughed again, showing his bloody teeth.

He reached for his waist, but Kidd was faster. He opened up Percy's chest at a range so close that blood dotted his black hoodie. When Kidd let off the trigger, Percy's chin fell to his chest. Kidd leaned toward the dead man and snatched the diamond chain from his neck. Behind him, Kidd smelled gas, and sure enough, Ollie had returned with a gas can. He tucked the chain in his pocket while Ollie poured it all over the house. When the two of them exited, Ollie lit a match and threw it. The remainder of the house was engulfed instantly in flames as they ran to where the car was parked on the next block.

"Whoo! That shit just gave me a fuckin' rush, man!" Ollie said when they reached a funeral home that Gene owned a ways away. "After we go holla at Gene, I gotta set me up some pussy for the night. You down?"

"Nah," Kidd said, throwing all of his guns into a duffle bag. He held the bag out to Ollie, and he did the same.

They'd parked in the back of the empty funeral home, and Kidd used the code to unlock the back door. Ollie grabbed a second duffle bag from the trunk of the car and followed Kidd inside. The first place they went was the bathroom. From the bag, Ollie handed Kidd some clothes and took his own into a separate stall. The two men stripped out of all the clothes they were wearing and changed. When they were done, they put the old clothing in the same bag as the guns, and Kidd took them to the crematorium while Ollie went to wipe down the car.

Kidd, in a fresh silk Gucci collared T-shirt and a pair of jeans, took his time. His thoughts were running wild, and he couldn't help but replay Percy's last words to him. What had he meant when he said to talk to his mother? And why had he said it? Kidd couldn't remember the last time he'd even heard her voice. Whenever he tried to visit her in the past, she denied his visitation form. Maybe it was out of shame, or maybe it was out of resentment. Either way, Kidd couldn't forgive her for it. At the end of the day, he was her son. Her flesh and blood. Nothing was supposed to be able to keep them apart, not even the walls of a jail. He'd believed her when she told him that she loved him, but after living without her for so long, he wasn't sure any longer.

Kidd finished doing what he had to do and went outside to join Ollie. He stood in the dark, staring at the car, and noticed that Ollie had removed the license plate from it. He smirked. Ollie loved that car, and he would cross all t's to make sure it wouldn't have to get burned after the job.

"You know you can't pull another job in this whip, right?" Kidd said, walking over to the passenger's side door.

"I know. I just wanted Sheila to experience one wild ride for the road. Feel me?"

"I feel that you're a whole fool," Kidd said, shaking his head. "Let's go tell this nigga the deed is done."

Gene was sitting at his dining room table, reading the paper and drinking coffee mixed with his favorite brandy, having a pleasant night. He was wearing his soft Versace robe over his pajamas and had a pair of slide-on slippers on his feet. His legs were crossed, and he was seemingly carefree. Marvin Gaye's voice filled the house as it played in the background as he read up on what was going on in the city. The mayor had approved a better meal plan for public schools, which was a shock because he had denied one for years. Gene smirked to himself, knowing that the mayor's favorite girl, Glitter, had something to do with that. The Bliss Lounge had a way of putting everyone in a good mood, so in a way, Gene felt that he was doing his due diligence for the city.

When he heard the front door to his home open, he didn't look up from the paper once, not even when he heard the footsteps approaching.

"It's done," he heard the voice of his nephew say.

"How do I know?"

There was a loud clanking sound when something was tossed onto the table next to Gene's coffee mug. Gleaming up at him was a diamond-studded necklace spelling out the word "God." With a straight face, Gene pointed to the corner of the dining room where two backpacks sat next to his fine-china cabinet.

"No point in counting. It's all there. Fifty thousand dollars apiece. And, Kidd, you are now officially off for a month."

"Thank you, sir," Ollie said, and he instantly went for the bags.

"No need to thank me. You did a fine job."

"You need a ride back to your spot?" Ollie asked Kidd.

"No, I'm good. I have my Jeep in the garage."

"All right, G. I'ma get at you later. Have a good night, boss."

When Ollie was gone and the front door shut, Kidd took a seat at the end of the rectangular table and faced Gene. The two men sat in silence for a while, and Gene noticed that Kidd hadn't made a move toward his money. He took a gulp of his drink and relished the warm feeling trickling down his throat.

"Is something on your mind, nephew?" he asked, flipping the newspaper.

"I'm just wondering what's so interestin' in the paper at this time of night."

"When you're a busy man like myself, you find that this is the only time to catch up on things."

"And what have you found out?"

"That some crazy woman drowned her baby in the tub, some woman opened a black-owned-and-grown grocery, and the mayor just approved a new meal plan for public schools this morning."

"Isn't the mayor a client of yours?"

"That he is."

"Hmm."

"What's that for?"

"I'm just wonderin'—"

"Seems you've been doing a lot of that lately."

"Maybe so," Kidd said. "I was just thinkin' that if you have all of these people in high places in your pocket, why haven't you used them to your advantage?"

"Use them to my advantage how?"

"Like try to get my mother out of jail."

On that last statement, Gene closed the paper and set it down on the table. He looked intensely at Kidd and tried to read his face, only to find out that he couldn't read his face. Kidd had always been a stony-faced kid, but right then, his expression seemed harder than usual.

"Believe me, I have tried everything to free your mother," he lied with a straight face. "But there are some things that are out of even my hands. Why are you suddenly interested in your mother's release? The last time you spoke about her, you said you didn't care if you ever saw her again."

"Maybe I've had a change of heart. I mean, she is my mother. Maybe it's time for me to hear why she wanted me to stay away for so long. I want to see her."

"She denied all of your visiting forms," Gene said with a smirk.

"I know you have enough pull to override that, Unc."

"Not to override prison protocol," Gene said, reaching into the pocket of his robe and pulling out a cell phone. "But maybe I can do something else for you." He dialed a number and pressed the phone to his ear for a moment. It rang a few times before the other end was answered.

"Hello?"

"Put her on the phone."

He heard shuffling on the other end of the line, but after about thirty seconds, he heard his sister's voice in the background.

"What do you want?" he heard her distant voice say to the prison guard.

"Telephone," the guard who was on Gene's payroll said. "Remember the rules and what will happen if you don't follow them."

Gene slid the phone over to Kidd, who hesitated a moment before picking it up and placing it on his ear.

"Hello?" he said into the phone, and Gene watched the hard expression on his face melt away within seconds. "Ma?"

Pause.

"Don't cry, Ma. It's okay," Kidd said and stopped to listen. "I know it's been a real long time. Why did you deny all of my visitation forms?"

Pause.

"You're my mom, man. I don't care what you look like. I just wanted to see you. How you been holding up in there?"

Pause.

"That's good. I miss you," Kidd said, and his voice cracked as he listened to whatever she was saying. "Nah, I could never hate you. I wanted to sometimes, but I could never really bring myself to. What?"

Pause.

"I haven't been over that way since Unc moved me in with him. I think they tore it down though."

There was another pause, followed by Kidd's laughter.

"I remember. You used to wear that tattered pink robe. That used to embarrass the hell out of me." Pause. "Okay. I love you too. I'm gon' do another visitation form, and you better not deny it. I need to see in person how you're doing. You might be lyin' to me or something. I love you."

Pause.

"All right, I will. Bye."

Kidd disconnected the phone and slid it back to Gene, who had been watching him like a hawk. His eyes were slightly glistening, but he wouldn't let one single tear fall. After all those years, Gia was still his soft spot.

"What did she say?"

"She just asked how I was and what ended up happening to our old house. She sounded pretty sad when I told her they tore it down."

"She didn't say anything else?" Gene inquired a little too eagerly.

"Nah," Kidd said and gave him a strange stare. "Why would she? And even if she did, I'm sure whoever you got on payroll in there will tell you."

Kidd pushed away from the table and got up to go grab his money. He patted his uncle on the shoulder in farewell and started toward the front door. Before he reached it, Gene called his name.

"What's up, Unc?"

"I need you to do one more thing for me before you go on your little hiatus."

"Like?"

"The tour bus gets back tomorrow right after noon. I want you to meet them at the Bliss Lounge and make sure everything is everything. And this new girl Aria was telling me about, you've met her, I suppose?"

"Yeah."

"And? Is she as beautiful as Aria says?"

Kidd shrugged his shoulders and looked over his shoulder at his uncle. "I mean, she's all right."

"Just all right?"

"Yeah," Kidd said and made a face. "All them bitches look the same to me. Fat booties, big titties, with just enough thought process to operate. That's how you like them, ain't it, Unc?"

Gene studied Kidd for a while, searching his face for any emotion other than the nonchalant one he was giving. When he couldn't find a lie, he picked up his paper and opened it to the spot where he left off.

"Hmm," was all he said. "All right, you can go. Lock the door behind you."

Chapter 11

Three can keep a secret if two of them are dead.
—Benjamin Franklin

Kidd couldn't get his mother's voice out of his head. He'd gone to sleep to her voice and woken up with it going off in his mind. She sounded so tired, not at all like she used to. She used to be so full of life and laughs. Fun should have been her middle name. She was the type of woman who was always on the straight and narrow. She wanted her son to go to Harvard and be the best he could be in life, which was why it was so confusing when she got arrested.

He lay in bed, that time alone, staring at the ceiling. He had one hand on his bare chest and the other behind his head. A few things weren't sitting right with him. One was that his uncle said he couldn't override prison protocol for a visit, yet he had somehow been able to get a call through whenever he wanted. The second was something his mother had asked about.

"How is the old house?"

When he told her it had gotten torn down, she didn't sound upset like he told his uncle. She was calm. She was also calm when she'd said, "Remember I used to check the mail in my robe every morning?"

Of all of the memories she could have brought up, why had she chosen the one he hated the most? Neighborhood kids used to give him hell behind that raggedy robe, but his mother refused to let it go. It had been her mother's before she died and it had sentimental value, she would say. Still, Kidd didn't care. It used to embarrass—

"The mailbox." Kidd cut his own thoughts short and sat up straight in his bed. "She wants me to go to the mailbox."

Of course, he couldn't be sure, but why else would she bring it up in such a way? Kidd thought about how intensely Gene had been watching him while he was on the phone and the questions he asked when he hung up. What if his mother was being forced to talk in code? But why? Nothing was making sense to him. The only thing he could do was go see if his assumption was right.

The digital clock on the nightstand read ten o'clock, proving that he'd been in bed for too long that morning. He was usually out the door by eight. Kidd stretched long and wide before stepping out of bed and placing his feet in his royal blue Armani slide-on house shoes. He walked over to the long window a few feet from his bed and opened his white drapes, welcoming the natural sunlight into the room before going to the bathroom. On his way, he turned on the sixty-inch television that was mounted on the wall in front of his bed so he could play some music while he showered. Opting for some slow jams, Kidd stripped and got in the shower.

He stayed in for almost thirty minutes before getting out and grabbing his outfit for the day out of his huge walk-in closet. He paired the cotton Burberry crew neck with a pair of Burberry tan slacks, finishing the look with a pair of matching loafers and a gold watch. Everything was brand-new, being that Kidd often bought more clothes than he could wear in a year. On his way out the door, he sprayed himself with cologne and brushed his hair. Before he left, he examined his lineup in the mirror next to his front door to make sure it was still crisp. When everything was satisfactory, he stepped out the door and couldn't help but think about what Belle would think when she saw him later that day.

Belle?

Was that why he wanted to make sure he was fly? In the back of his mind, he knew the answer, but he would never admit it to himself. There was no telling what Aria had her on that tour bus doing, and he was almost positive that the Belle he left wasn't who was coming to Miami. Still, a piece of him yearned to see her. He hadn't heard from her since the day he'd gone out to eat with Ollie, although he had reached out a few times. He decided to just let it go. Kidd, however, opted to drive her Camaro so that way she would able to get around while in Miami.

On the ride to his old digs, Kidd wondered if it was a good idea to drive near the crime scene he'd helped commit. Curiosity got the best of him once he arrived in the neighborhood, and he couldn't help but drive by Percy's old spot. There were police everywhere, and the remains of the house had yellow tape all around it. Kidd slowed the car by one of the neighbors across the street standing outside, looking at what was going on outside his house.

"Excuse me, sir," Kidd said to get his attention. "Do you know what happened over here?"

"Man, it was crazy!" the older, plump guy said. "Somebody blew the house up, man. There were a bunch of motherfuckas inside, too!"

"Damn, that's crazy. Does anyone know who did it?"

The man looked down at Kidd and raised his eyebrow high to the sky. "You ain't one of them cops, is you? 'Cause I ain't no snitch, and ain't nobody finna come after me and my family."

"I look like twelve to you?"

The man eyed Kidd for a little longer until he was seemingly satisfied that the person in the car wasn't the police.

"There are speculations goin' around, but nobody knows for certain. The fella who owned the place musta used it to move dope, if you ask me. Always had somebody outside watching the front and scoping the neighborhood out. Shit, whoever done blowed them boys up did the neighborhood a favor. We already got so much to deal with, we don't need that shit too."

"Thank you," Kidd said, somewhat satisfied with his answer.

He rolled the window up, but not all the way, before he drove off. It was a nice day, and he was enjoying the breeze on his face. He rounded a few corners until he came upon his house, or at least the plot that his old house used to be on. Ollie's old house was still standing. Some foreigners had moved into it and were outside sitting on their porch. They watched Kidd curiously when he parked the car by the curb in front of their house and got out. He ignored them and went to stand in front of where the house he grew up in used to be. He knelt down and let the old memories he'd suppressed come flooding back. He had forced himself to forget them when he thought his mom forgot about him. But right then he remembered just how great of a mom she'd been to him.

He stood up straight, thinking about what she'd said, and looked toward where the mailbox used to be. It was still there. He guessed the city didn't see the need to rip the mailbox up from the ground. Kidd went to it and opened it, expecting to see nothing but spiderwebs, but there was something there. It was a small, folded-up piece of paper with his first name written on it. He quickly looked around him, as if whoever had left the paper were still around somewhere. All he saw were the Taiwan people looking at him as if he didn't belong in his own neighborhood. Removing the paper, he unfolded it and read what was on it.

Your mother wants you to speak with me. I can explain everything. Call me.

There was a number listed at the bottom of the paper that Kidd didn't recognize. There was no signature, just those words that he read over and over. He clenched his jaw, not knowing what to make of it, before folding it up and putting it in his wallet. He checked the gold Rolex on his wrist and realized that it was time to head over to the Bliss Lounge. He got back in the car and hit the highway, hoping he would beat the bus there.

He didn't know what to expect with Belle, but he hoped that she wouldn't make the decision to officially become one of Gene's Girls. He meant the last words he'd said to her. And while they were said in a place where lust could overtake any man, they had come from the heart. He would rather see her anywhere else than the Bliss Lounge. There were only a few things that a working girl could get from there, and happiness wasn't one of them.

When he'd taken on the security job for the club, he hadn't counted on feeling compassion for the girls. Maybe that was why he felt such a strong need to protect them. But when it came to protecting them from Gene, even he was powerless. All it took was one mistake to get on his uncle's bad side. Kidd had seen his share of body bags. He'd even helped dispose of some of the girls' bodies. He was sure if the girls knew exactly what they were signing up for, they wouldn't have inked their names on the contract. Because once they did, Gene owned them. Mind, body, and soul.

Kidd had wanted to tell Belle that the last time they spoke, but like Aria, his loyalty was still shifted too much toward Gene. Now he wasn't so sure. There were too many questions surrounding his uncle. He thought about the piece of paper in his pocket and contemplated whether he was going to use the number listed. He couldn't lie and say he didn't want to know who had left the letter and how they knew he would go and get it.

Before he did something he would regret, Kidd thought it was best to tread lightly for the moment. One hurdle at a time. The first was to make sure Aria hadn't completely brainwashed her new recruit the way she'd done to so many others. She pretended to be their friend, to gain their trust. And once she had it, it was too late for the young women. They'd already been caught in the spider's web.

But that time he thought things would be different. He'd gotten the vibe that Aria really liked Belle. She didn't act the way she had with any of the other girls. Not as pushy. Not as fake. For the first time in a while, Kidd had seen the real soft and caring side. But then again, maybe she had just gotten better at being deceptive.

Because at the end of the day, Gene always came first. He couldn't help but wonder if Aria knew that Gene had been searching for Belle, or if she had just gotten lucky. Either way, whatever Gene had planned for Belle wasn't good.

Kidd didn't understand Aria's loyalty to Gene. He knew Gene had found her while she was practically starving on the streets, but that still didn't explain it to him. She would have given her life up for Gene with no question or hesitation. What he said was law to her, and it was like she lived to grovel at his feet. And if groveling meant bringing him the freshest meat on the block, then so be it. Kidd should have told her no when she asked if she should let Belle on the tour bus, but he'd been so mesmerized by Belle that he just couldn't let her go. Maybe that was why he felt it was his duty to relieve her of Gene's Girls. Because if she went down that road, he would be partly responsible for whatever her fate would be.

Chapter 12

Diamond, diamond, diamond, diamonds on me dancing.
—Future

The tour had come to an end for the winter season, and Belle found herself wondering what was next for her. In such a short amount of time, she'd saved up a little over $50,000. That last night in Atlanta had been a killer. She'd made $15,000 in one night. She had more than enough to start fresh somewhere and never look back. She couldn't see herself going back to Nebraska, not anytime soon anyway. That was the place where her heart broke, and she needed to be somewhere that would heal it. And she didn't know how long that process would take.

She sat cross-legged on the bed in the tour bus with Cream and Dynasty passed out asleep beside her. Cream's face was still busted and bruised, so she was forced to sit out the last tour stop in Atlanta. As Belle watched her sleeping peacefully, she felt a strong empathy toward her and wanted to stroke Cream's face the way her mother used to do to her when she was upset. Maybe Russian was right and this life wasn't for her. She didn't want to end up like Cream. Not now, not ever. If what Russian Roulette said was true, Aria would turn on her in a heartbeat once her name was on the dotted line. Her mind was made up.

Belle listened to the sound of giggles coming from the front of the bus where everyone else was. The girls were up there playing some card game with the security and sounded like they were having the time of their lives. When Kidd left, Belle didn't bother getting to know the person who replaced him. She just let them all do their jobs without getting in their way.

After the first day of texting Kidd, Belle had stopped replying to him, although she was the one who had initiated the conversation. There was something about him that made her want to push him away. Because if she didn't, she would pull him as close to her as she could. The way he cared about her well-being was something that she didn't feel she deserved. Mentally she was weak, and emotionally, she was broken. If she was damaged when she first started the tour, she was certainly damaged goods now. He'd watched her sell her soul for money. How could he ever want her? Still, the look in his eyes when he looked at her the night before he left lingered with her. If she hadn't been so high, she probably would have left with him. But she was too stubborn.

"You all right back here?"

Belle realized that she had been staring into space, but she quickly snapped out of her daze when she heard Aria enter the room. They hadn't really spoken since the night Cream got hurt, and in truth, Belle had done her best to stay out of Aria's way. She just couldn't look at her the same. Even in that moment with Aria dressed in a dark blue skintight T-shirt and a pair of Bermuda shorts, all Belle saw was Lady Passion.

"Belle, are you all right?' Aria repeated. "You've been awfully quiet."

"I'm good," Belle said and cleared her throat after hearing how meek she sounded. "Just a little tired, that's all."

"Aren't we all?" Aria said and sat down at the vanity. "I really wish you had been with us at the start of the tour. I know you made some bread, but if you had been on the whole tour with us, you would be coming back to Miami with at least two hundred thou. You'll see for yourself next time."

"Next time?" Belle found herself asking, and she could have kicked herself.

"Yeah." Aria looked at her in the eyes. "You don't plan to stick around?"

"I haven't figured it out yet," Belle answered truthfully.

"Beauty, you just made a motherfucka's salary in a few weeks, and you want to give that up?"

Belle gave her a funny look. Aria had called her by her stage name, the same as she did with the other girls. When she thought about it, Belle hadn't heard Aria ever call them by their real names, and vice versa. Russian Roulette's voice snuck up on her again.

"You're a good girl, Belle. Smart, sweet, compassionate. But Lady Passion only sees your face and your body."

"Earth to Beauty," Aria said and snapped her fingers.

"Belle," Belle told her, looking sharply back at her. "My name is Belle. We aren't in a party. Call me by my first name."

Aria opened her mouth like she wanted to say something, but she quickly shut it. Belle saw her jawline pop out as she clenched her jaw. Maybe she didn't like the tone of voice that Belle used with her, but Belle really didn't care.

"Okay then, Belle," Aria said, adding extra emphasis. "I hope you aren't planning on leaving us. There is a lot more money to be made."

"I haven't decided yet," Belle answered, still looking Aria in the eye. "I'm not sure if this is the right thing for me. After all, I don't want to end up like Cream."

"So that's what this is about? That's why you've been so quiet?" Aria said and chuckled.

"I heard you beating her," Belle said since the cat was out of the bag. "She was begging you to stop, but you just kept going. You beat her like she was a dog."

"What happened to Cream is what happens when it comes to light that over ten thousand dollars' worth of Miami's finest dope has been getting snorted up her trifling nose. Trust me, she's lucky I found out about it and Gene didn't, because I could have easily made a phone call. And if I had done that, something much worse would have happened. Gene doesn't take too well to being taken advantage of, especially by people he puts in a position to become rich. So what if they have to use their bodies to do it? They signed a contract, and until that contract is up, they know the rules."

"They. They. They," Belle said. "The girls this. The girls that. What about you, Aria?"

"What do you mean?"

"You barely dance, yet you're on the tour with the rest of the girls. How do you get paid?"

"I guess there were a few details I left out in the beginning, but only because I didn't want you to think I asked you on board for personal gain."

"Details like?"

"Like, as Lady Passion, I already receive a set amount of earnings from the Bliss Lounge for coming on this tour. And when we get back, every girl is to pay me ten percent of her earnings."

"Wow," Belle scoffed. "Is that why you wanted me to come with you? You saw me and thought about how much money I would make you? I should have known it was too good to be true."

"No, that's not it," Aria said, shaking her head with distraught eyes. "I didn't plan on taking any of your earnings. I didn't want to do anything to discourage you from becoming one of us."

"So that I would sign my name on the dotted line. Then you could make money off me the next time around."

"No." Aria stopped talking to close her eyes and take a deep breath. "That's not what I meant, Beauty."

"My name is Belle!" Belle snapped.

The bus began to slow down, and the driver yelled back to them all that they had arrived at their final destination. Belle's things were already packed up next to her duffle bag of money, and she grabbed them as soon as she felt the bus come to a complete stop. She'd officially made her mind up. The moment she got her car from Kidd, she would be back on the road again. Before she rushed to the front of the bus, she stopped and looked down at Aria's pitiful face.

"I appreciate you for giving me this opportunity, but this is my last stop."

With that, she left the room and made her way to the front of the bus. The other girls were rushing toward the room to grab their things, so she had to bully her way out. Finally, though, she was able to get off the bus and step into the warm Miami sun.

She turned in a circle and took in her surroundings. They were parked in the back of a sleek, tall black building. The windows were tinted, so she couldn't see inside at all, but she was almost certain that you could see out of them. There was a door that led inside of the building back there with a key card entrance, but Belle didn't even want to see the inside of the place.

There were no other businesses around it in her eyesight's range. In fact, it felt like she'd been dropped off in the middle of nowhere. Her eyes travelled over every car in the parking lot as she searched for her own. There were so many cars there that it took a while, but finally, she spotted it near the back, gleaming in the light like it had just been washed. She was able to take only one step toward it before a voice stopped her.

"Going somewhere?"

She didn't recognize it, and when she whipped around, she knew why. She had never in her life seen the middle-aged man standing on the sidewalk. The door she'd seen earlier was now wide open, and two big, burly guys wearing suits stood on either side of it. The man who was looking directly at her too was wearing a tailored suit and looking like a million bucks. He was handsome and clean-cut, and Belle didn't have to be close to him to tell that he probably smelled delightful. In between the pointer and middle fingers of his left hand was a Cuban cigar, or she assumed it was. She doubted a man of his caliber smoked anything other than the finest.

"Gene?" she asked with a level of uncertainty in her voice.

"What gave it away?" he joked with a charming smile. "Now what are you doing looking like a mouse ready to run away from a cat."

"I . . . I was looking for my car," she said.

"Ah, yes. The Camaro my nephew has been driving around."

"Nephew?" Belle questioned. "You're Kidd's uncle?" Kidd hadn't said anything about Gene being his uncle.

"I'm sure he didn't tell you. He's a very private person if you don't mean anything to him," Gene said casually and waved for her to come closer to him.

There was something entrancing about him, because she felt her feet move toward him without question. When she was near enough, she inhaled his scent. She had been right to assume he smelled heavenly. He examined her face, and his eyes didn't drop beneath her collarbone. They didn't need to. He was sure to have seen every curve she had to offer in her formfitting maxi dress when she walked toward him.

"You're even more ravishing than I was told," Gene said, gently placing a finger underneath her chin and lifting her head ever so slightly. "A woman of your sort should always keep her head high. You weren't planning to leave so soon, were you?"

"I—"

"Good," Gene said with a smile. "Follow me inside the Bliss Lounge while the others are unloading. Bring your things with you."

He turned and walked back in the door he'd come out of and didn't look back, as if there was no question that she would follow. And there wasn't. There was an invisible string that Gene pulled her with, and she went after him with her bags in tow. She walked through the doors and matched him stride for stride down a long, dark hallway. When finally the room opened up, she had to do a double take because she was blown away. She literally had to clamp her lips shut to stop herself from uttering, "Wow," at the sight.

"This is the main hall," Gene said and waited for one of his security detail to unhook the barrier separating the exit from the rest of the vast room.

The Bliss Lounge was something from a movie. The main hall was one big room that resembled a Las Vegas nightclub. There were big black leather couches and glass tables on top of the red carpet that set the tone with the jet-black walls. There were no windows in the main hall, but there were staircases that led the patrons to different levels of the lounge all over. There were many stages and completely naked women dancing seductively on them. Some twirled on poles while others captured their prey on the ground. At that moment, although it was only midday, the place was swarming with people enjoying the environment and snorting as much cocaine as their hearts desired. The soft music that graced the air was the same music the women were dancing to.

"Drink?" Gene offered and held a hand toward the long bar.

Belle glanced over and saw another naked woman behind the bar staring curiously at her. As many naked women as she had been seeing the past few weeks, one might have thought it would be normal to her by then. Still, Belle found her eyes on the woman's extra-large breasts. They were so big that Belle couldn't understand how she was still standing. Her back had to have been killing her.

"Uh, no, thank you," she answered. "Not right now."

"All right, well, how about we go to my office then?"

"That's fi—"

"Unc?"

Upon hearing the voice, Belle whipped her head around and saw Kidd standing right there. The butterflies fluttered into her stomach without warning. He was even more handsome than the last time she saw him, and she found herself tucking a piece of her hair behind her ear. His eyes were on her like it was the first time he'd ever seen her, and there was a fire shooting to the center of her face. She recognized a look of concern in his eyes when they shifted from her to Gene.

"Hi," was all she could come up with to say.

"What's up, Belle. You all right?"

"Yeah, I'm good," she answered.

"Okay," he said. "I'm glad to see you made it back in one piece. Your whip is outside, and the keys are on the dashboard. I put a couple of miles on her, but she still drives smooth."

Next to her, Gene looked from Belle to Kidd curiously. When Kidd noticed, he returned the stare and added a little iciness to his. They held their glares for a few moments before Gene cleared his throat.

"Have all of my girls gotten off of the bus?" Gene asked him.

"Yeah. Phil is taking it to get cleaned now."

"Good. And where are the girls?"

"In the count room, getting ready to pay Lady Passion her cut of the tour."

"Very good."

"Did you need me for anything else?" Kidd asked.

"Actually, yes," Gene said, looking back to Belle. "I was just about to take Belle here to my office, but come chat with me for a moment. Fellas, why don't you show Belle to my office."

"Okay, boss," one of them said and motioned for Belle to follow them.

With one last look at Kidd, Belle complied and left him and Gene behind. The two burly security guards led her through a few doors until they reached a spiral red carpeted staircase. Once they went up it, there was yet another hallway, that one shorter than the rest with a gold door at the end of it. When they got to it, one of the men opened the door for her to go through, but they didn't go in after her. Instead, one flicked the overhead light on while the other pointed at a chair.

"The boss will be in shortly."

"Well, what am I"—the door slammed before she could finish her sentence—"supposed to do?"

They didn't hear her question because they were gone. Belle sighed and let her duffle bag fall from her shoulder onto the ground. She looked around the big office and knew instantly that Gene had a severe God complex.

On two of the four walls were two big murals of himself. It went without saying that they were beautifully painted. Still, it was a little much. The room was set up almost like a king's chamber, and on either side of his desk were two tall golden lions facing her, almost like they were guarding something. She contemplated snooping through his things but thought better of it. The hairs on the back of her neck were standing straight up, and just in case she was being watched, she thought it was best to do what Gene's security said.

Keeping the duffle bag of money close to her legs, Belle sat down and waited patiently for Gene to come into the room. She just hoped that he took it well when she told him that she would be leaving. If what Aria said was right, she would hate to see what happened to anyone who got on his bad side.

***

"What's going on, Unc?" Kidd asked, but Gene ignored him to wave to the bartender.

"Thunder!" he called.

"Yes, sir?" she answered in a sweet voice.

"Bring my nephew and me two rum and Cokes, please."

"Of course, sir."

"Sit," Gene instructed.

Kidd did as he was asked and sat in an empty booth with his uncle away from everyone else. He couldn't tell by the way Gene was looking at him what he was thinking. It, however, was a stare that made him uncomfortable. Just as he was about to break the ice, Thunder had come over with their drinks.

"You know I love my girls, right?" he said to her as she served them.

"Yes, Gene," she said with a robotic smile.

Her breasts were so big that they were close to both men even while she stood an equal distance between them. Thunder was a nicely shaped white woman who tanned so much she was probably giving herself cancer and she didn't realize it. Her dark hair draped over her shoulders and brushed her bare backside. The six-inch stilettos she wore made her body sit up in all the right places and made her butt seem plumper than it actually was. She stared lovingly down at Gene like he was her lover and made sure he had extra napkins with his drink.

"Do you belong to me?" Gene asked her and took a sip of his drink.

"Yes, Gene."

"Are you happy here?"

"Very happy, Gene," she told him with a concerned look. "Have I done something wrong? Am I in trouble?"

"No. No trouble at all," Gene said, reaching to touch one of her nipples. He pinched it ever so slightly and bit his lip when he saw the hint of pleasure enter her eyes. "I'm glad I can make you happy. You can go."

Upon exiting, she took Gene's hand in hers and kissed the rings on his fingers. When she sashayed away, Gene watched her until she was back at the bar. He smirked to himself and turned his attention back to Kidd, who hadn't touched his drink at all. "You know what I like most about the Bliss Lounge?"

"What's that?" Kidd humored him.

"Everybody knows their place."

"Really? I heard you had a little run-in with something like that while I was gone."

"Oh, you mean Anthony? Well, he quickly learned what happens to those who mix what's supposed to stay apart," Gene said, giving Kidd a knowing look. "As they all do."

"'What's supposed to stay apart.' You say that like you own these people."

"I employ them. Same difference. While inside or affiliated with the Bliss Lounge, they are mine. Speaking of affiliated, is there a reason why you downplayed Belle to me when I asked about her last night?"

"I don't know what you mean," Kidd said, finally taking a gulp of his drink.

"I mean, why didn't you tell me what kind of man trap she is? She has a face and a body worth millions. Not at all just 'all right' as you like to put it."

"Maybe I didn't look at her like that."

"How did you look at her then?" Gene asked, and Kidd saw that he'd fallen into a trap. "Did you look at her for her brain? Or her intellect? Or maybe she made you laugh while you were on tour with her. Maybe . . . That's the reason you left the tour, isn't it? You started liking this girl Belle, didn't you? Couldn't stand to see Lady Passion turn her into what you knew she'd become."

When Kidd didn't object, Gene's eyes opened wide, and he wagged a finger at him. The satisfied look on his face made Kidd want to slap it away, but he couldn't. Everything Gene had said was right.

"Dear boy, there's so much you need to learn. What you are feeling toward her is an infatuation that only a beauty like that can bring. What have I taught you?" he asked and waved around toward all the naked women around them. "All women are whores. They are all disposable. As a man, you need not get attached to one when you can have them all."

"What are you going to do with her?" Kidd came right out and asked.

"With Belle? Why, I'm going to offer her a new home. Being that she doesn't have one."

"No," Kidd corrected with a scornful chuckle. "Being that you murdered her whole family."

"Correction, that was Percy, not me."

"Same difference. He was there on your orders. Regardless of how it happened, their blood is on your hands."

"Either way, the fact is that she needs a home. And what is a better place to call home than the Bliss Lounge?"

"You've already destroyed her life."

"I'm giving her a new one."

"And then what? You're going to drug her up and keep her high as a damn kite so she doesn't even know you're using her to get what belonged to her father?"

"Enough!" Gene commanded. "It's clear to see that this girl has you wide open. You're talking to me like you have a big-ass pair of balls between your legs, but need I remind you who the fuck I am? Belle is no longer your concern, and due to that big bag of money she brought in, she's also now off-limits to you. Any hope of getting your dick wet is out the window. If I find out you've been anywhere near her, I'm going to forget that you're my nephew, and you'll find out what happens to those who cross me. Understand? Now, aren't you on break? Get out of my sight."

Kidd answered him by knocking his glass violently to the ground, shattering it and causing glass to go everywhere. A few of Gene's security started to approach them, but Gene held up a hand to stop them.

"No, let him go. My nephew is just having a bit of a temper tantrum right now."

Kidd glared at them all before standing. When his eyes fell on Gene's face, it didn't feel like he knew him at all. Percy whispered in his ears like a ghost haunting him.

"He'll take anybody out who gets in his way. Even you."

Kidd turned his back and stormed out of the building. His entire body was on fire, and there was no amount of water that could have put him out. It wasn't until he reached the parking lot that he remembered that he had driven Belle's car there and didn't have a way to get back to his condo. He thought about calling Ollie, but he didn't feel like being bothered with his happy-go-lucky friend.

"Fuck!" he shouted and punched the air.

He plopped down on a random car and looked to the sun. He hadn't felt a gush of anger that big since the day he saw the federal agents take his mother away. Suddenly he remembered the piece of paper in his wallet and pulled it out. He stared at it for a few moments before deciding to call the number on the bottom.

"What the hell," he said. "I have nothing to lose."

He dialed the number and placed the phone to his ear, listening to it ring. He was just about to hang up when somebody on the other end answered.

"Hello?" a woman's voice answered.

"Who is this? I found this note at my old house. Did you leave it there?"

"Andrew?" the person asked, and that proved that she knew who Kidd was.

The only problem with that was that he didn't know who she was.

"Who is this?"

"I can't say over the phone. Is there a place I can meet you?"

Kidd paused, not knowing if it was a setup. Gia was his mother, but it had been too long since he'd seen her. Still, she was his mom. He had to hold on to the hope that she wouldn't snake him. He looked around at the nothingness surrounding him. Gene had chosen the most rural area he could find in Miami for the Bliss Lounge, knowing that the nearest building, a gas station, was about an hour's walk down the road.

"Yeah," Kidd said finally. "Can you meet me in an hour?"

Chapter 13

*Greed is a bottomless pit which exhausts the person in
an endless effort to satisfy the need without
ever reaching satisfaction.*

—Erich Fromm

"I see you've made yourself comfortable."

Gene's voice startled Belle, causing her to jump in her
seat. She hadn't even heard him come in the office behind her. He shut his office door behind him and went to
sit behind his desk. She didn't know what to do or what
to say, so she did and said nothing. She felt as if his eyes
could read every movement of her face, so she sat as still
as possible. There was something about him that made
her spine tingle and not in a good way. He was every
meaning of the word "intimidation." It didn't matter if
the expression on his face was a kind one. He had a lethal
aura hanging all around him.

"Do you want something to drink?" he asked courte-
ously. "If you don't want an alcoholic beverage, I have
some waters in the fridge behind me."

"No, thank you. I'm fine," Belle declined even though
her mouth was drier than the Sahara Desert.

"Suit yourself," he said and smiled. He didn't say anything else. He just kept looking at her in a way that made
her fidget.

"Is there a reason you asked me to come up here?" she asked when he didn't speak for a few moments.

"You really are stunning. Do you know that?" Gene asked, ignoring her question.

"I've been told."

"Your whole life?"

"Most of it."

"Good. How was your time spent with my lovely ladies?"

"It was good."

"Good, not great?"

"Well, I never danced before," Belle said. "I mean, in the club with my old friends from college. But never . . . like this."

"Really?" Gene said and somewhat raised the skin on his forehead. "To my knowledge, you were quite good at it."

"Pleasing a roomful of drunk and high men wasn't too hard."

"Interesting. Did you make a lot of money?"

"Yes."

"And how much did you make?" Gene asked.

"About fifty thousand dollars."

"Whoo! Fifty thousand bones, huh? Wow. There's somebody out there who doesn't even make that per year's salary, and you did that in a few weeks."

"Yeah," Belle said and glanced over her shoulder at the door.

"Well, I can see that you're in a rush to leave, so I'll cut straight to the chase. I'm assuming that while on tour with the girls you've learned a little bit about how the Bliss Lounge works."

"I've learned enough," Belle told him. "And I don't want to sign a contract. I don't want you to own me for five years, or ten. So if that's why you called me up here, I just can't do it. I'm sorry. I just want to go on about my life."

There. She'd said it. The worst was out of the way. Still, watching Gene's blank facial expression made her feel like she was waiting for a great white shark to attack. His lips were in a straight line, and the look in his eyes was a menacing one. Belle was almost certain that she was about to die, but then something appalling happened. Gene smiled so big that she swore she could see all of his teeth.

"Then I guess you're in luck. If you leave, I will grant you the courtesy of letting you take all the money you've made with you after Lady Passion gets her small fee," Gene said, getting up from his chair.

"Th . . . thank you," Belle said, shocked.

"No, I should be thanking you. To be in the same room as something so exquisite has certainly made my day. I can see why my nephew took a liking to you."

"Oh, I don't—"

"Please," Gene said and held his hand up. "That is none of my business. You're free to go. Be sure to see Lady Passion on your way out."

Belle couldn't believe it, but he didn't have to tell her twice. She grabbed the small suitcase with her clothes in it by the handle and placed the duffle bag over her shoulder before standing up. She sashayed over to the door and was just about to place her hand on the handle.

"But before you absolutely make up your mind, might I ask, what are you going to do when that runs out? Because it will run out and you'll be back at square one."

His words made Belle stop in her tracks. She could see her own puzzled expression in her reflection from the gold doorknob.

"I know that by now, my girls' luxurious lifestyle has rubbed off on you. The shopping sprees, the five-star restaurants and hotels. Are you really ready to go back to living a regular life? Having to pinch pennies just to make sure you don't deplete your savings too soon? But even if you do that, even if you get a job, no amount of money is going to come in faster than you spend it. Unless, of course, you stay. I can assure you that you'll be taken care of and you'll have more money than you can count in a day's time."

Belle slowly turned back around to face him. The expression on his face showed that he was genuinely concerned about her well-being. But how could she be so sure? Maybe it was an act.

"You say that I will be taken care of, but what you really mean is someone will be watching me at all times. I don't want to live life like that, and I don't want to be under contract. I would want to be able to leave whenever I wanted to."

"And I can make that happen for you. You don't have to sign a contract to be employed by the Bliss Lounge. However, it would always be my duty as the employer of something so fragile to keep security around you. Even if you choose to live off-site, security detail is something that is not up for debate. You want to leave with fifty thousand from two weeks' time. If you stay, I can guarantee you double that in two weeks. I can also promise you that nobody will lay a hand on you."

There was something about the way he added that last part that made her look over her shoulder at him. Her jaw tightened as she remembered Cream's face when Aria was done with her. There was something Aria said, the day she caught Russian Roulette on the bed talking to her. Something that had stuck with Belle.

"And if I say no?" she finally asked, staring intensely with her amber eyes.

"I don't think you want to," Gene said.

"I can't say you're lying," she said, and he smirked. "But I have one condition."

"That is?"

"I want to be a lady. Lady Beauty."

Chapter 14

The truth is rarely pure and never simple.
                                            —Oscar Wilde

By the time Kidd got to the gas station, he was a hot, sticky mess. The sun was glaring down on him the whole time, and he was positive his already-brown skin had gotten even darker. On the way, he'd removed his shirt and used it as a rag to wipe the dripping sweat from his face. He got a few weird stares when he walked up to the gas station in a wife beater with a gun on his hip, but those people weren't his focus. He was there for a reason. The person on the phone had told him to look out for a gold Lincoln Navigator, and sure enough, when he arrived, there was one waiting for him.

Upon approaching the car, he prepared himself for what he might find when he opened the door. The windows were darkly tinted, so he couldn't see who was driving. That made him more cautious. The doors unlocked when he got close enough to grab the door handle, and he placed his other hand on his hip. He opened the door, and when he saw who was driving, his mouth almost hit the pavement.

"You?" he asked, astonished.

It was Luella, the server from the restaurant. Except right then she wasn't the server from the restaurant. She was his contact. She was wearing a plain pink blouse and a jean skirt with her hair pulled back. When she saw him standing there looking at her with a dazed and confused expression, she returned it with a look of annoyance.

"Yes, me. Now get in this car before these crackers call the police on your ass for comin' up here with a gun!" she exclaimed. "I swear, your mama told me you were smart. Tuh! Please."

Kidd did as she said and got in the car. She pulled off before he'd even shut his door all the way. She hit the road, playing her old music, and constantly checked her rearview like she was making sure nobody was following her. Kidd was still shaken up and didn't know what to say, but Luella had a mouthful.

"And why on earth would you have me pick you up down the street from that son of a bitch's establishment?"

"You mean Unc?"

"No, I mean that son of a bitch!" Luella let him know that she meant what she said.

"I wasn't in my car when I got there."

"You ain't never heard of Uber?" she asked, looking at him like he'd come from a different planet. "No matter, I think we're good. I don't think anybody followed us."

"Why would anybody follow us?" Kidd asked, finding himself shooting a glance to the back window of the truck.

"Because they don't want you to find out the truth, that's why."

"The truth?"

"Yes, the truth. Ain't you hear me, boy? The truth!"

"The truth about what?"

"About your mom. She's watched at all times. That's why she had to tell you to go to that mailbox in code. I left that message there even though I told her you probably would never find it. I guess you are kind of smart," Luella told him. "You ain't never wondered why she didn't want to see you? You never wondered why she denied all your attempts to visit her? It wasn't because she didn't want you to see her like that."

"Then what was it? What other reason could keep a woman away from her son for almost ten years?"

"She was keeping you safe," Luella said.

"Safe from what?" Kidd inquired.

"Where do you live?" Luella asked and put her hand up as if to stop him from talking. "These years haven't been that good to me. I feel old as a bat. I can't do all this talking and driving now. I'll explain everything once I can sit on a couch and have a glass of sweet tea."

Twice in a row, somebody had silenced him like he was a little boy, and it wasn't sitting right in his chest. He had half a mind to tell her to pull over and take her advice about getting an Uber, but that would defeat the purpose of calling her in the first place. Plus, he was curious to know exactly what she was talking about.

"And put your damn seat belt on, boy! You're gonna get me a damn ticket!"

Kidd glared at her and mumbled something under his breath. He did what she said, though. The ride to his condo seemed to last longer than it actually was. He didn't know if it was the music or the smell of lavender that made it drag on, but whatever it was, he could have leaped for joy when they were finally in his parking garage. He exited the truck first and then helped her out before leading the way to his place.

"Well, I'm glad to see that you have some manners at least," she told him when he held the door to his condo open for her.

"You know, you were a lot nicer at the restaurant."

"Yeah, well, I get paid to do that," she said and winked at him as she walked past.

He locked the door behind them and went into the kitchen to see if he had any sweet tea in the refrigerator. By the time he brought it to her, he saw that she made herself comfortable in his living room on the couch. He handed the teacup to her with a couple packets of sugar.

"Just in case that's not sweet enough for you," he said and took a seat next to her.

"Thank you," she said, taking a sip of the tea. "Mm, mm, mmmm! That's good right there. Did you make this?"

"Yes, ma'am. My mom loved her some sweet tea."

"I know that's right. Gia would drink a whole gallon if you let her," she said with a fond smile.

"How do you know my mom exactly?"

"We went to college together. We were like two peas in a pod back in those days. Well, three. You do know she went to school in Atlanta for a bit, don't you?"

"Yeah, I think I remember her telling me that."

"Yep. Those were the good ol' days," she said and continued sipping her tea.

Kidd waited for her to bring up what she was talking about in the car, but when she didn't do so on her own, he initiated the conversation. "What did you mean in the car when you said my mom wanted to keep me safe? Keep me safe from who?"

"Who do you think?"

"I don't know. That's why I'm asking you," Kidd said, feeling himself growing agitated.

"From that monster of a man you call your uncle."

"Uncle Gene? That doesn't make any sense. He took me in after she went to jail."

"Did you ever wonder why?"

"I guess I just always assumed it was because he was my uncle."

"Ha! You mean to tell me that you think Gene Hightower committed a selfless act?" Luella asked and gave a deep, hearty laugh. "Everything that man does is strictly for personal gain."

"What could he have possibly gained by welcoming me into his home and taking care of me?"

"Your mother's control," Luella said, looking into Kidd's eyes. "Tell me, what do you know about the reason your mom is in jail?"

"She was laundering money and got caught in the act."

"Laundering money?" Luella asked and laughed again. "That's what they told you? I can tell you're a smart boy, Andrew, so I know you can't possibly believe that. How could she have done that? Through the hospital job she was working?"

"Okay, well, if that wasn't it, what was it? Because that's what Uncle Gene told me."

"Well, your Uncle Gene is a lot of things, but a truth teller isn't one of them," Luella said, setting her cup down on the glass coffee table in front of them. She turned back to Kidd and grabbed his hands in hers as if to steady him for what she was about to say. "A little over ten years ago, your uncle came up with this crazy idea for a gentlemen's club. He wanted it to be away from everything and everybody to make it more exclusive, and he found the perfect spot for it. The only thing was, the property and the land was already owned by a guy named Miguel Torres. Miguel didn't want to sell to Gene."

"But he got the land," Kidd said, butting in. "Somehow he got the land, right? What did he do, blackmail him?"

"Worse," Luella said, shaking her head. "See, blackmailing him would have been too easy for Gene. Where is the fun in that? No, Gene set him up and used your mother as bait."

"Why would she do that?"

"You were a growing boy, Andrew. He promised her enough money to take care of you for a long time if she lured Miguel away from a bar and back to a hotel. Gene killed Miguel that night, but not before he tortured him into signing over the deed to the land and building. That murder was traced back to your mother months later."

"And he let her take the fall for him?" Kidd asked incredulously.

"Yes," Luella said. "And he threatened that if she ever told the truth, he would kill you. That's why he made her deny your visiting requests."

There was an anger welling up in the pit of Kidd's stomach that he'd never felt before. It was pure rage. For so many years, his mother had had to sit and rot in prison alone because of something Gene talked her into doing. Not only that, but Kidd had hated her for so long, not even knowing that she was just trying to keep him out of harm's way. He couldn't imagine the feeling of knowing that the only way of keeping your child safe was to push him away. The agony knowing that the person she was trying to keep her son safe from had him nearby at all times. Gene had mentally tortured his own sister for years to command her decisions. For that, he would have to pay. Kidd tried to pull his hands away, but Luella didn't let them go.

"That's not all," she told him.

"What could be worse than finding out you've hated your own mother all these years for nothing, Luella?"

"Gene is planning something, Kidd."

"Gene is always planning something."

"No, something bigger." Luella shook her head. "Gia told me the other day when she called me after Gene visited her."

"Gene visited her?" Kidd asked and suddenly remembered the day Gene had him and Ollie waiting at his house. "What did he want?"

"Information about the husband of our other close friend from college."

"Who?"

"Her name was Taina. She was a real looker, too. So beautiful. She married well. A man named Lucas Dubois."

"Wait, did you say Lucas Dubois?"

"You know him?"

"I know of him. Gene—"

"Got him and Taina killed," Luella said, and tears flooded the corners of her eyes. "They didn't deserve that. They were good people."

"They had a daughter who survived," Kidd told her.

"Thank God," Luella said. "And hopefully Gene never finds her, because if he does, the world is in trouble. Gia thinks that he wants to use the Bliss Lounge to control everyone in the country who has a voice. Lucas's company represented everyone from musicians to politicians. All it takes is one trip to his little gentlemen's club to have them wrapped around his finger. But without the sole owner of Lucas's company, Gene won't have access to any of the information he needs. He doesn't need that kind of power. Nobody needs that kind of power."

"Shit," Kidd said to himself and tried to iron out his thoughts. "His brother. Lucas had a brother. Somebody needs to have him tighten up security and tell him what's going on so he knows." There was a sadness that came over Luella's gaze that was hard to miss. "What's wrong?"

"Oh, baby. He's already dead. Murdered last night. It's been on the news all morning."

"But Gene was here in Miami last night."

"Gene has long money, baby. Just because he's here doesn't mean he can't reach elsewhere," she said.

"Then that means Belle is the only one left," Kidd said and looked at Luella and slumped his shoulders in a defeated fashion. "Gene already has her."

"What? How?" she exclaimed.

"It's a long story." Kidd shook his head. "But she's at the Bliss Lounge as we speak."

"And you just left her there?"

"How was I supposed to know all this shit?"

"Well, you have to go get her. Your uncle is a dangerous man. You should know. You're one of his hired hands. You know what happens to people once Gene has no use for them anymore."

Her revelation took Kidd aback. "How do you know about what I do?"

"Come on, boy. Do you think that just because your mom is locked up, she didn't at least keep tabs on her baby boy? She's proud of you. I hope you know that."

"Even though I didn't go to Harvard?"

"I'm sure she is, but just in case, you can make it up to her by doing one thing," Luella said, staring deeply into Kidd's eyes. "Save that girl, and put an end to Gene Hightower."

Chapter 15

Love can only be found through the act of loving.
—Paulo Coelho

In the weeks that followed, Belle grew accustomed to her new life in Florida. It was a different kind of vibe than the one she was used to. Life in Nebraska hadn't been too slow, but compared to Miami, it was a snail. She moved into a nice-sized apartment in a good area in town. She decked it out to her liking, which meant the color pink was everywhere. Pink drapes, pink rugs, pink wall décor. She'd chosen off-white furniture, and her bedding was the color of opal. It wasn't anything like the home she shared with her family, but it would do for the time being. She had a neighbor she'd started getting to know named Char, who seemed cool. Belle thought that it would be nice to have a new friend who wasn't a stripper.

Gene had kept good on his promise and granted Belle the title of Lady Beauty. He also did not require her to sign a contract with the Bliss Lounge under the condition that she pay weekly dues while she worked there. To top it all off, he also allowed her to pick her own schedule. She could go in and work only one day a week if she wanted to, but Belle had grown money hungry. There was barely a day that she didn't show up for work. If she missed a day, all she thought about were the Benjamins she would miss out on.

There was one strange thing about working for Gene, and that was that she barely ever saw Kidd. Now that she knew he was Gene's nephew, it was even stranger, because she knew he was around somewhere. Whenever she did get a glimpse at him in the lounge, he would be gone before she got another. She tried to contact him again, but all she got was a message back saying the number had been disconnected. She was positive that the last time he looked at her, she saw something there. Something more that she couldn't explain because it was more so how she felt. She tried not to let it bother her. Maybe it was best to just forget about him.

That night, she was cursing herself as she walked down the steps of her apartment because she'd taken a little longer on her makeup than she wanted to. There, of course, was a room at the Bliss Lounge that the women used to get dressed, but Belle preferred to walk in with her face already beat. That way, all she had to do was get dressed and go. The yellow midi dress she wore hugged her curves tightly, but she could still feel her butt bounce with each switch. The three-and-a-half-inch nude ankle strap heels she wore gave her a comfortable lift, and her pretty polished toes gleamed in the moonlight.

She was almost to her car when she heard footsteps approaching her, but she didn't stop walking. The hairs on the back of her neck stood up, telling her that something wasn't right, but still, she did not look back.

"Where you going, walking so fast?" a gruff voice said close behind her.

The owner of the voice grabbed her forearm tightly and spun her around. Belle turned her nose up instantly, seeing a man in his thirties with hair and a beard that badly needed a trim. He was brown skinned, dressed like a thug, and not attractive to her eyes at all. The man was standing a little too close to her, and Belle had to take short breaths to not inhale too much of his liquor stench. He wasn't alone, either. Not too far behind him were two more men, each looking at Belle with the same lustful gaze. Belle had no idea where they came from, because they surely weren't from around there. All three of them had golds in their mouth that made their teeth seem like they hadn't been brushed in weeks, and it made Belle want to gag. She tried to snatch her arm away, but he had a tight grip on her.

"Where you goin' dressed like that?"

"How about you just let my arm go so I can get there?" Belle snapped.

"Damn," he said, licking his crusted lips. "Hot and spicy, just like I like 'em. You got the body of a dancer. Is that what you is? You a dancer?"

"Nigga, let me go," Belle demanded. She tried to yank her arm away again and failed.

"What?" he said with a grin. "You don't like me or somethin'?"

"Ay! Y'all leave her alone!"

Belle looked up and saw Char standing on her porch. Char was wearing an oversized T-shirt that hid her curves and whether she was wearing any shorts underneath. On her feet were a pair of furry slides, and she had thick rollers in her weave. Belle felt a surge of relief wash over her when she saw her neighbor.

"Bitch, go back in the house!" the man who was holding on to Belle said.

"Scoop, stop it," Char said, calling the man by name. "Y'all was supposed to wait for her to leave."

Belle realized what was happening, and her relief was short-lived.

"We were, but you ain't tell me how scrumptious she was," Scoop said and turned back to Belle. His eyes fell on her perky breasts and stared at her erect nipples before looking back in her face. "Char already told us that you was a dancer, so you ain't even gotta answer that for me, sweetheart. Now, why don't you be a team player and tell us where the cash is at?"

"Not in my apartment if that's what you thought," Belle said. "If y'all were waiting until I left to rob me, y'all were going to be highly disappointed. Ain't shit in there but maybe some expensive fine china and designer clothes. That lick wouldn't have even been worth it."

Scoop eyed Belle's face hard before breaking into a sinister grin. "Well, that's too bad, isn't it? But I still want to find out myself," he said.

"You'll be wasting your time," Belle said firmly.

"Well, say I am wastin' my time tryin'a go up in your spot. What you say you, me, and my niggas here climb in your car and have some fun? Call it even."

It was then that Belle regretted lying to Gene and telling him she was staying with Dynasty. Well, she really hadn't lied, because that was where she was laying her head until she got her place. She just failed to mention that to Gene. She planned to, but she wanted to enjoy the little privacy that she had for a little longer. She looked around, but there was nobody in the parking lot to witness what was going on, and if anyone was looking out of their window, they didn't seem to care.

"In your dreams," Belle said. She pushed on Scoop's chest and finally broke free. "I'm not a prostitute."

"You're right about that," Scoop said and pulled a chrome pistol from his hip. "'Cause prostitutes get paid, and you gon' pay me. You either gon' take us to the money or pay the fee in pussy. Or maybe you wanna pay with your life. What will it be?"

He raised the gun and pointed it at Belle's forehead. Flashbacks of that night at the gas station came to her, and she remembered how it felt to have unwanted hands roaming her body. She would rather die than sell her soul, and Scoop found that out when she spit in his face.

"You bitch!" he exclaimed, raising a hand to strike her.

Boom!

The gunshot sounded so close that Belle was certain somebody had shot her. But when she looked down, she was still in one piece. Looking at Scoop, she saw a look of pure terror frozen on his face as he looked at something behind her. She turned around to see Kidd walking toward them with a still-smoking gun hanging at his side.

"What's good, Kidd," Scoop said, and Belle noticed that the bass in his voice had vanished.

"Ay, G, what the fuck y'all doin' over here, man?" Kidd asked, stopping next to Belle. "Holding a gun to one of Gene's girls like you lost yo' fuckin' mind?"

Scoop's eyes widened, and he looked back at Belle. "Aw, man. I didn't know she was one of Gene's," he said and held his hands up. "I wouldn't have even tried her if I had known. My cousin just said a stripper with lots of cash moved across the hall. We was just tryin'a hit a lick, that's all."

"Sounded to me like you were about to do more than just rob her," Kidd sneered, raising the side of his lip. He held his gun up to Scoop's face and put a finger on the trigger. "Fuck is wrong with you niggas? Out here takin' pussy like a bitch. Give me one reason why I shouldn't smoke you in this parking lot."

Scoop didn't say anything. He was frozen still. He probably hadn't even realized that his gun had dropped to the ground as he was staring at the pistol in his face. Belle swore she didn't even see his chest moving, like he was holding his breath, and that made her angry.

"So you're only big body with females, huh?" she asked and slapped him so hard that her arm instantly became numb.

Kidd's head jerked in shock, but he didn't stop her from giving him an ass whooping of a lifetime.

"Ah ah," he said, aiming his gun at the two minions behind Scoop when they looked as if they were going to help their partner. "Y'all know who the fuck I am and how I get down. I wish you niggas would lay a hand on her. I'll leave your brains on the concrete. Drop your guns on the ground."

They did so without so much as a complaint, and when Belle was done with Scoop, Kidd hit him so hard with the butt of his pistol that a few teeth went flying.

"Ho-ass nigga," he said when Scoop fell to the ground. "Every time you look in the mirror now, you'll think of me. And understand that the only reason I'm lettin' you leave here with your life is because I already know there are witnesses waitin' on a homicide to happen. But know you're on borrowed time. Get the fuck out my face."

Kidd let Scoop and his people go but didn't let them grab their guns. He intensely watched them run, stumbling, to a baby blue Dodge Charger and speed off. He had put his gun away, but his fists clenched in a way that let Belle know he didn't really want to let them get away. She bent down to pick the guns up and went to a nearby sewer drain, tossing them down. When she got back to where Kidd was standing, she caught him looking toward her apartment complex.

"That nigga said his cousin lives here. You know her?" he asked in a dry tone.

"Y . . . yeah. She's my neighbor."

"Show me."

"Are you gonna hurt her?" Belle asked.

"Maybe."

"Right this way then."

She led Kidd from the parking lot and back to the apartment and showed him the exact apartment that Char stayed in. The hallway had high ceilings, as did the apartments, and smelled delicious like someone had made a home-cooked soul-food dinner that evening. The hallway was brightly lit, and it was quiet, being that the other two apartments were on the lower level of the building. She pointed at the door across from her own apartment, letting him know that was the one. She thought he was going to knock, but with one swift movement, Kidd kicked the door in. Belle followed closely behind him, and they saw that Char had been in the middle of rolling up a blunt in her living room when she heard the loud noise. She instantly reached her hand under her couch cushion, but Belle's fist to the side of her face stopped her.

"And here I am thinking you were cool," Belle said, unleashing all of her anger on her. "You were going to just let them rob me and rape me, huh? Is that what you were gonna do?"

Belle's fists plummeted into Char's defenseless face until she had blood leaking from nose and mouth. The only reason Belle stopped was because the adrenaline rushing through her veins was making her heart pound violently, and she needed to breathe.

"Get out," Kidd told Char simply.

"This . . ." Char huffed. "This is my shit. You can't make me leave."

"I can when my partner is the landlord," Kidd said. "You're evicted, effective immediately. Now get the fuck out. I'm not gon' ask you again, bitch."

Char looked from Belle to Kidd and weighed her options. Finally, she grabbed her Coach purse and got to her shaky legs going to the broken door. Blood drops stained the sandy brown carpet with each step she took. Belle hit her a few more times when Char passed and shoved her as hard as she could to the ground.

"Y'all are dead," she said when she picked herself up. "I'ma make sure of that."

Kidd didn't seem at all affected by her words. He watched her until she left, and when she was gone, he asked Belle if she knew what kind of car she was in.

"I think a yellow Jeep," she told him, looking at the broken door. "You aren't worried about what she just said?"

"Nah," Kidd said, shaking his head. "She ain't gon' make it to see the morning. None of them are."

The way he said it, Belle believed him. The fear in Scoop's face when he saw Kidd spoke volumes. He almost peed himself. Belle studied the hard expression on Kidd's face as he stared into space. She hadn't ever seen him that mad, but she wasn't afraid. She cleared her throat and interrupted his thought process to point at the door.

"What you gon' do about that?" she said. "I ain't paying for it."

"Don't worry about that. My best friend Ollie owns this property. It was one of the first things he purchased when he started gettin' bread. He'll have somebody come take care of it," Kidd said. "Go wash that blood off your hands. You probably need a shower, too."

Belle looked down, and sure enough, she had drying blood all over her knuckles. There were even a few splatters on her dress, and she groaned. "I really liked this dress."

"Go 'head. I'll meet you over there," he said.

"What are you about to do?"

"I need to make a phone call."

Belle didn't ask him to elaborate. The less she knew, the better. She glanced down at the time on her phone and saw that it was almost eleven o'clock and got irritated. She was missing out on money because of the stupid stunt those nobodies tried to pull.

Once inside her two-bedroom home, the first place she went was to the master bathroom. When she was done washing every trace of blood from her skin, she kicked her shoes off and plopped down on her bed.

"Dammit!" she shouted and punched her comforter.

"Chill out, shorty, they're gon' get handled," Kidd's voice entered the room. "Believe that." He leaned on the doorframe and observed her.

"That's not why I'm mad," she said to him. "I'm missing out on money because of this shit."

"Of course that's what you're worried about," Kidd scoffed.

"What's that supposed to mean?"

"Nothin'. That was just fast is all."

"What was fast?" Belle said, quickly growing tired of his game.

"You turnin' into one of them."

She didn't have to ask him to elaborate to know exactly what he was talking about. She jerked her neck at him before looking him up and down. "I didn't turn into anything but a woman who's about her money."

"There it is, that stripper attitude."

"You don't even know what you're talking about," she said, rolling her eyes.

"Don't I? I've seen it too many times. The sweet, innocent girl turnin' into money-hungry smut. That's how it always happens. I don't know why I thought you would be different."

The disappointment in his eyes made Belle's stomach drop. She hated how he was staring at her. Not with anger, no. That wasn't what she saw in his eyes. It was pity.

"Okay, you spoke your piece. You can leave now," she snapped.

"Damn, you're not even gon' give a nigga a thank-you? If it weren't for me, those dudes would have had you pinned down somewhere."

"I can handle myself," she said and pulled a small Barretta from the Gucci handbag she was carrying. "I would have handled it."

"You're carrying guns now?"

"Yep."

"Since when?

"Ever since Gene told me to start carrying one."

"Does Gene control everything that you do? Speakin' of Unc, doesn't he usually have somebody for any girl who lives off-site?"

"Mind your business. And I'll mind mine."

"He doesn't know you don't live with Dynasty anymore, does he?"

"No. And to answer your question, nobody controls me," she told him. "And how did you know I was staying with Dynasty? Matter of fact, how did you know where to find me? The only person who knows that I was even looking at this place to move was her."

"Maybe I put a little bug in her ear when she let it slip that you were stayin' with her but lookin' to move," Kidd said. "Maybe I'm the one who suggested this place."

"And why would you do that? Matter of fact, why are you even here?"

"Because I wanted to see you."

"I don't see why. I haven't seen you in weeks."

"Gene doesn't like it when business and pleasure mix, so I had to keep my distance for a while."

"Why did you want me to move here then?"

"So I could keep my eye on you."

"From a distance?"

"Right."

"Well, I don't need you to watch me anymore, okay?" Belle snapped.

"You sure about that?"

"Yeah." She paused and furrowed her brow at him. "Wait, what do you mean, mix business and pleasure? You and I have never done anything."

"It doesn't matter. If Gene even thinks somethin' is goin' on, there will be hell to pay. He's very possessive over what he thinks is his," Kidd told her, coming into the room and kneeling in front of her. "He's done unimaginable things to men he's employed for dabbling in the amenities of the Bliss Lounge."

"Is that why it was so easy to keep you away from me?" Belle's voice had dropped to just above a whisper. His nearness gave her butterflies. She could smell the cologne radiating off of him, and the way her bedroom light hit the diamonds on his chain made it look like he was literally shining. Her head dropped, but his finger caught her chin.

"Stop playin' with me," Kidd told her. "You know I feel somethin' for you. And I think you feel the same. I hope you feel the same, anyway. Do you?"

"I don't know," she told him. "I don't even know your real name."

"But you know my heart," he told her. "If it makes you feel any better, it's Andrew."

"That doesn't do me any good now."

"I'm sorry, Belle. I stayed away to keep you safe."

"Keep me safe from what? I don't think Gene would hurt me."

"It's complicated," Kidd told her and shook his head. "You don't know my uncle the way I do. And if somethin' were to happen to you, I'd torch that place to the ground. I don't know what kind of spell you cast on me, Belle Dubois. Since the first day I met you, you've had me wide open. And I don't even know what the pussy is like."

Belle's hands seemed to have a mind of their own as they traveled up and over Kidd's blue Balenciaga shirt. The fabric was smooth underneath her palms all the way until she got to his neck and face. She didn't break eye contact with him when her fingers wrapped around the back of his head.

"I do feel the same," Belle told him. "I don't know what it is, but I do know that you saved me that night y'all found me. And ever since I only feel safe when I'm with you."

"I don't want to be the reason you get hurt," Kidd told her. "I need to keep you safe until I iron some shit out."

He tried to pull away, but she had a firm hold on him. Even so, he didn't try very hard. He was caught in her trap.

"If you leave, I don't know when I'm going to see you next," she said. "Stay."

"You need to go to work, remember?"

"I can miss tonight."

"You haven't even gotten in the shower."

"Clean me."

Kidd couldn't hold her off anymore. Or it might have been that he couldn't hold himself back. Their lips found the other's, and they shared a long, deep, passionate kiss. Their tongues danced beautifully, and neither of them cared to come up for air anytime soon. Kidd's hands fondled her breasts and pinched her nipples through her dress before ripping the thin fabric at the bust.

"Mmm," Belle moaned into his mouth when her breasts bounced freely.

Kidd wrapped his arms around her waist, picking her up. She wrapped her legs around him and let him carry her into the large, well-lit bathroom. When he set her down, he turned the shower on before turning back to her. He then finished ripping her dress until she was completely naked, and when she was, he stepped back and looked at her.

"What?"

"You're everything," he told her and caressed her cheek. "Do you know that? You are the most beautiful woman I've ever seen in this lifetime."

Belle smiled. She'd heard that sentence so many times, but that was the first time that it meant something. Her clit responded to the way he was eyeing her down, and the place between her thighs became soaked with her juices.

"Take these off," she instructed, pointing at his clothes.

She helped tug his shirt over his head and unbuckled his jeans so that he could kick them off. The bulge in his briefs was impressive, but when he removed those too, she bit her bottom lip. She took a deep breath as she grew even more aroused. Stepping into the hot shower water, she motioned with one finger for him to join her. When he slid the door closed behind him, she wasted no time dropping to her knees and staring his thick, eight-inch snake in the face. Her lips were around its head in seconds. She didn't care that the water was destroying her freshly flat-ironed hair as it rained down her body.

She gripped his sides with her hands to keep him steady as she forced his manhood to the far back of her throat. The sound of the shower became just background noise as her gurgles and slurping took over the room. She made love to him with her mouth, and by the way his legs shook, she knew he loved it. In her mind, his skin tasted like her favorite milk chocolate Hershey bar, and she couldn't get enough. She would have kept going until he shot his kids in her mouth if he hadn't forced her up.

"You tryin'a have me goin' crazy," he growled in her ear and pinned her to the wall of the large shower. "I know that's what you were tryin'a do. You tryin'a have this dick crazy about you, huh?"

He grabbed a handful of her hair and roughly pulled her head back so he would have access to her neck. His lips and tongue sampled her neck and travelled down, pausing at her nipples. Volts of electricity coursed through her body, making her jump whenever she felt his teeth take a nibble.

"Oooo," she moaned and let her left hand fall between her legs while the other dug into his shoulder. "Baby. That feels so good."

She used her middle finger to swirl around her engorged clit while he feasted on her breasts. Kidd's hands massaged her butt cheeks like he was molding clay, and just feeling his strength mixed with his wet tongue was enough to bring on her first orgasm.

"Ahhh!" she shouted into the showerhead like a microphone.

"Let me taste," Kidd demanded and lifted Belle in the air.

Her back slid up against the wall, and he placed her thighs on his shoulders. With a small hum, Kidd buried his face into her kitty cat before her climax had passed all the way. Her face twisted into a grimace, and she tried to steady her breathing as his tongue beat away at her throbbing clitoris, but it was impossible. She cried out over and over but never once told him to stop. Her hands caressed the top of his head and encouraged him to keep sucking and licking away like she was his favorite candy until she sprayed him with more of her juices. Her entire body vibrated, but he wasn't done with her yet. He let her slide down but not so her feet were touching the floor. He made her wrap her legs tightly around his waist again. Kidd kissed her tenderly, and she kissed him back.

"Mmmm. Mmmm," she moaned with her arms around his neck.

She held him tight like he might disappear at any moment. She wished there was a cameraman to capture that beautiful scene so that she could really hold on to him forever. The tip of his manhood positioned itself at her slippery opening, and Belle gasped as it fought against her walls for entrance. Her nails dug into his back at the pleasurable pain, and with three powerful strokes, Kidd gained access to her most secret fortress. Everything around Belle faded to black as Kidd drilled into her, and the only thing she saw was him. His rough breathing into her ear turned into small moans, and Belle could hear her wetness mixing in with her own cries of bliss. She worked her hips to meet him stroke for stroke. Just as he was fucking her crazy, she wanted to do the same to him. Their eyes connected, and in that moment, they were one. Kidd's wet hand found her face, and he rubbed her lips before he rammed into her deeply.

"This pussy," he said and shook his head and suddenly withdrew.

"What about it?" she said breathily, grabbing for him when he set her down. "Why'd you stop?"

"It's dangerous," he panted. "Don't let me back in it unless you plan to give it to me forever."

His words went straight to her chest. She could tell by the fierceness of his gaze that he was dead serious. The shower water ran down his face and onto his muscular torso, giving him the look of a Greek god. He was more than a man. He was her man. Or at least she wouldn't mind him being that. She stood on the tips of her toes and kissed his soft lips before pulling away and turning around. Placing her hands on the soap holders for balance, she bent over, giving him the best view of her round butt and swollen kitty. Looking back at him, her amber eyes pierced his.

"You can have it as long as you want it," she said. "Just don't leave me again."

"I promise," Kidd said, gripping her hips and sliding back in her warm gooeyness.

Her words must have turned him on something vi-
cious, because his strokes had a different kind of power
behind them. She couldn't even throw it back. All she
could do was take his beating. It felt so good, and all
of her senses were awakened. Her toes curled, and her
eyes clenched shut. When Kidd used his middle finger to
anally penetrate her while fucking her silly, Belle started
saying words that didn't even exist. She screamed over
the sound of his balls slapping into her skin, and her
clit welled up, letting her know it was time for another
release.

"Cum with me," he told her when her knees started to
buckle. "I'm about to cum, Belle. I'm about to nut all in
this pussy."

"Ahhhh!" Belle's scream was her response.

The eruption that came from her clit was as strong
as the throbbing from Kidd's shaft inside of her when
he let go of his seed. His fingers dug into her side,
and his entire body shook from his climax. When the
crazy sensation subsided, Belle dropped to the floor of
the shower. She had exhausted all her energy and could
barely move. She let Kidd wash them both up and let
the now-lukewarm water rinse the soap from their bodies. When he turned the water off, he wrapped her towel
around her and carried her to her bed. She didn't know
what happened next because she lost consciousness.

Belle stirred in her sleep before she opened her eyes.
The sun sneakily peeked in at her, almost as if it didn't
want to disturb her beauty rest. And it didn't. The television on her wall was what interrupted her dreams. She
gave a long stretch and a big yawn before sitting up in her
bed. She realized that she was still naked, but she didn't

mind it because her silk sheets were so soft on her skin. Events from the night before snuck into her mind, and she smiled while touching her cheek. She had never experienced sex so good in her life, and when she smelled the bacon coming from the kitchen, she smiled even harder because she knew Kidd was still there. Just as she was about to toss the covers back and grab her robe, something on the television caught her attention.

"The deaths of the entire Dubois family have left the city of Omaha shattered," a Fox News anchor was saying. "As we found out a few weeks ago, taking Lucas Dubois, his wife, and his young son was not enough for the killer. It is speculated that the same assailant came back a few weeks ago and murdered the new CEO and owner of Dubois Enterprises, Karan Dubois. Detectives are working long and hard to figure out what may have triggered these murders. In the meantime, the fate of Dubois Enterprises is in the balance."

Belle stopped tuning in after that. The only thing she'd heard was that her uncle was dead. Whoever had killed her mom, dad, and brother had gone after Uncle Karan too. And that meant he could be after her next. The room was closing in on her, and she was finding it hard to get air to her lungs.

Kidd entered the room with a plate of freshly made breakfast. The smile on his face vanished when he saw Belle in bed, hyperventilating. He set the plate of food down to rush to her side.

"Belle, what's wrong?" he asked in a panic. "Breathe, baby. What's wrong?"

"The news. They just . . . said . . ." She tried to speak, but her heart was pounding too hard.

"Breathe, baby girl. Take your time."

"My uncle is dead," she finally got out. "Whoever killed my family must have gotten to him too."

"I know," Kidd said plainly.

"How could you possibly know?" she exclaimed. "Oh, my God. What if they're after me next? Oh, my God, Oh, my God. I'm going to die."

"No, you aren't," Kidd said. "I'm not going to let him hurt you. I'm gon' protect you. I'm going to kill him before he gets the chance."

"How can you protect me if you don't know who's doing it?" Belle asked and tried her best not to go into another panic attack. "My parents were killed ages ago. If the police can't find the person, what makes you think you can?"

Kidd's lips formed into a grim straight line when he looked at Belle. His eyes held a look of sympathy. No. Not sympathy. Regret.

"Belle, I have to tell you something. I have to tell you the real reason I came here last night," he started. "It wasn't just to see you. There's somethin' else. But first I need to ask you some questions."

"What?"

"When Gene offered you the job at Bliss, what all did he have you do? Did he have you sign anything?"

"He didn't make me sign a contract," she said. "I told him I didn't want to be in one. I saw Aria beat Cream up so bad, I just couldn't see myself being bound to that for any time frame. I want to be able to leave when I want."

"He didn't make you sign anything?"

"I mean, some insurance papers, or at least he said they were insurance papers. They had my name and social security number on them, so I believed him."

Kidd looked at Belle and shook his head. "It didn't strike you as odd that a man who had never met you before had that kind of information about you at his fingertips?"

"I guess I didn't think about it."

"Belle, those weren't insurance papers. You signed your father's company over to him."

"What?" Belle said and made a face. "That doesn't make sense. My uncle is the owner of the company, not me."

"Was the owner. He's dead now. When he died, you became the rightful owner of Dubois Enterprises. And because you signed those papers, now Gene is."

"But that doesn't make sense," Belle repeated. "Why would he want my dad's business unless he . . . Oh, my God. Gene killed my parents. . . ." Her voice trailed, and she looked at Kidd with tearful eyes. "Did you know?"

"Not at first."

"You brought me right to him, you son of a bitch! You brought me right to the man who killed my family! Was this your plan all along?" Her screams were followed by her swinging at him with closed fists. She got a few hits in, but he grabbed her by the wrists. "Let me go!"

"Belle, listen to me," he pleaded. "I wouldn't do that to you. Me meetin' you was completely by chance. All this other shit is just proving that our paths crossing was fate. You have to believe me."

"What does he want with my dad's business?"

"All of his clients. Lucas Dubois represented some pretty powerful people. I think he wants to use Bliss to get them in the palm of his hand."

"Or blackmail them into it."

"That too."

"Your uncle is the devil," she sneered.

"I know it, and that's why he has to be stopped before he can do anymore damage. You have to trust me."

"And why would I do that again, Andrew?"

"Because Gene took somethin' special from me too. He's the reason my mom has been locked up for ten years. I hated her for so long because I didn't know the truth. That truth was that Gene made her take the charge for somethin' he did. All so that he could open his stupid club in the first place."

"Why didn't she ever tell you?"

"He threatened my life if she ever spoke to or saw me."

"Damn." Belle cupped his cheek with her hand. "You haven't seen your mom in ten years?"

"Nope. Gene stole her from me. And because of that, he's gon' pay with his life."

"Are you going to kill him?" she asked, thinking about her family's lifeless faces.

"Yes," Kidd answered bluntly.

"When?"

"It's gotta be tonight. I can't sleep another night knowin' he's still breathin' after what he did to me."

"I want in," Belle said flatly. "I want to help."

"I can't let you do that, Belle. It's too dangerous."

"That monster took the things I loved most from me," Belle said, blinking her tears away. "You don't have a choice. Please."

They stared at each other in silence for a few moments, and Belle let the tears fall freely from her eyes. Kidd grabbed her softly by her arms and pulled her into him, holding her tight. When he let her go, he nodded and kissed her forehead.

"All right," he told her. "Do you work tonight?"

Chapter 16

Power tends to corrupt, and absolute
power corrupts absolutely.
                                    —John Dalberg-Acton

"'Oh, baby, love and happiness . . . Love and happiness, oh!'"

Gene sang loudly along with Al Green in the back of the Mercedes-Benz limousine. He was in the best mood, and he could say that he looked as good as he felt. As usual, he wore a tailored suit, a deep burgundy that time, and had a glass of champagne in his hand. He was on his third glass, but who was counting? It was a time to celebrate. His future was shining so brightly that it blinded the past.

Aria sat across from him in the limo, holding her own glass of champagne. The time read almost nine o'clock at night, and Gene made it his business to personally pick Aria up. At first, she thought she'd done something to displease him, but then she saw the limousine outside waiting for her. She didn't know what to think, and still didn't. She was watching Gene like he was an alien from outer space. She'd never seen him act the way he was acting, let alone seen him sing a song.

"Are you okay?" she asked.

"Am I okay? I'm great! And it's all thanks to you, Lady Passion," he said, beaming at her.

"Well, you're welcome?" she said, not understanding what he meant. "I don't know what I did, though."

"Just know that you brought me the final piece to my puzzle," he said and held his glass in the air. "A toast!"

She held her glass up as well and clanked it with his.

"Cheers to the never-ending money flow bestowed upon the Bliss Lounge."

"I can definitely cheer to that," Aria said with a grin.

They downed their drinks together, and she set her glass to the side. He, however, poured himself another glass. "You have been my most loyal girl since the beginning, you know that?"

"I do," she answered and looked at him with cat eyes. "Which is why I was a little confused to find out that you gave Beauty the title Lady."

"Bitter are we now?" Gene asked, clearly amused. "I got the vibe that you looked at her kind of like a little sister."

"I do, but that doesn't mean I want to share my job title with her. She doesn't even know what she's doing. She's too scared to put the other girls in their place. Her leniency is going to cause insubordination, and I won't have that. I've worked too hard at whipping those bitches into shape. I like her, but that can go out the window fast."

"Don't you worry your pretty little head about Beauty. She won't be working in the lounge for much longer."

"What do you mean? Are you going to—"

"Kill her? Heavens no. That would be a waste of such an amazing being," Gene said with a mysterious smile.

"Then what are you going to do? Fire her?"

"No. I don't want her out of my sight. Ever. I'm going to make her my woman."

"What?" Aria said, looking into Gene's handsome face with a flabbergasted expression. "But . . . but what about me?"

"What about you? You just said that you want to be the only one with the title of Lady, and I'm giving you that."

"No, that's not what I mean. I've been here since the beginning, Gene. I deserve to be your woman!"

Gene burst out laughing like Aria had just told the funniest joke in the world. He laughed so hard that tears came from his eye. He grabbed the handkerchief from the pocket of his suit and dabbed the corners of his eyes.

"Now that was funny," he said and drank the rest of his drink. "What would ever make you think you deserve that?"

"I've slaved myself for you, Gene," Aria said, and her words came out sounding like a plea. "I make sure that everything at the lounge runs smoothly. I've recruited more girls than I can count. Everything I do is to keep you happy. I've killed for you, Gene. I have blood on my hands for you, and I would do it again. I love you, Gene."

"As you should," he said, setting his empty glass down. "But why would I want someone like that as my woman?"

"Someone like me? I'm loyal."

"No, all I heard was you telling me how weak you are. Your loyalty is a hindrance. I need somebody who can think for herself. All you do is say yes."

"Because I love you!"

"You don't love me, because you don't even love your- self. Look at you. If I told you to lick the bottom of my shoe, you would," Gene chuckled. "But Beauty? Unlike you, she has a spine."

"You bastard," Aria said and instantly regretted it.

Gene came across from his seat in seconds and had his arm on her throat. He pressed so hard that her airway was completely blocked, and he didn't stop, not even when she began clawing and hitting him.

"Don't ever for a second think that you are better than any of those other whores I have working for me," he sneered into her ear. "The only thing you're good for is pussy and the allure of pussy just like them. So it will do good for you to learn your place. I own you. Mind, body, and soul forever. Don't ever forget that."

He let her go, and she clutched her neck, gasping for air. Gene glared at her as he went back to his seat. He was angry that she'd ruined the great mood he was in just minutes prior. She was pathetic, and that was why she would never be anything more than what he had made her. And he could show her better than he could tell her.

Gene unzipped his pants and pulled out his erect penis. He looked maliciously at her. He wasn't just her boss. He was a master who commanded her without words. Leaning back into the leather seat, he watched her get to her knees in the limo. The moment he felt her lips wrap around the tip of his penis, he threw his head back in bliss. Not from the wetness of her mouth, but because of the control he had over her. Life was good.

Chapter 17

The future is uncertain, but the end is always near.
—Jim Morrison

"Lady Beauty in the house!"

"Yesss! I love the hair!"

"Lady Beauty, you are the fairest one of us all!"

The ladies in the dressing room all called out to Belle as she walked through. She couldn't blame them, though. She'd pulled out all the stops that night. She wore a black dress with wide horizontal cuts across it, and underneath, she had on a lime green bra. Her hair was pulled up into a tight ninja bun with choppy bangs, and her eyelash extensions were long and wispy. Her makeup was flawless, and she'd settled on a smoky eye with a natural lipstick on her full lips.

A few of Gene's clients had requested her company the moment she'd gotten there, so she'd been keeping pretty busy. It was a Saturday night, so the place was booming with those who had flown in from out of town to live out their fantasies. Anyone who wanted to see Belle dance had to pay a pretty penny and were also on a strict "no touching" rule. It was easy money for Belle, and she liked it that way. The men didn't seem to mind. Just being in her presence seemed to be enough for them to empty their pockets.

"Y'all are too sweet," Belle said and took a seat behind a vanity.

She was so busy looking at herself in the mirror that she didn't even notice Aria sitting at the vanity next to her. As usual, she was dolled up wearing a sexy gold lingerie set. That night she wore the matching silk robe to go it. Things between them had been weird ever since they had gotten to Miami. Now that Belle was a Lady, she understood why Aria had done what she'd done to Cream. Granted, she couldn't see herself beating anyone, but there were a few incidents with the girls where she wanted to smack fire from them. She turned toward Aria and tried to offer a kind smile.

"I heard Russian Roulette's last day was last week. What do you think she's doing with herself?"

"Who knows," Aria said, not looking her way.

"Well, whatever she's doing, I hope she's happy."

"What do you care? The only person you care about is yourself."

"Excuse me?" Belle asked and almost jumped when Aria whipped to face her.

"You think I don't know what the fuck you're doing, bitch? After everything I did for you, this is how you repay me?"

"Aria, I don't know what you're talking about," Belle said, truly clueless.

"Of course you don't," Aria said with an evil glare. "Well, since you don't, let me lay it out for you. You wanted my title, and now you want to be Gene's girl."

"Aria, when I asked to be a Lady, I just said that because I didn't want to dance as much," Belle answered honestly. "And I thought we were all Gene's Girls."

"You know what I mean! His actual girl. His woman!"

"What?" Belle asked, but before Aria could respond, Drip came and interrupted them.

"Lady Passion, the governor is here," Drip told her. "He only wants to see you."

"I'll be right out," she said, and Drip walked away.

"Aria—" Belle tried, but Aria held her hand up.

"Only speak to me if absolutely necessary," she said, and with one final glare at Belle, she was gone.

Her words didn't sit right with Belle. Why did she think Belle wanted to be Gene's woman? Even before she knew what she did at that point in time, she would never want that. Gene was handsome, but she could never see herself with him. Not with somebody like Kidd around. Her thoughts tried to consume her, but the cell phone vibrating in her Chanel fanny pack put a stop to that.

"Hello?"

"Gene just went up to his office. Now is the time," Kidd's voice said on the other end.

"Okay. I'm going now."

"Remember the plan. Stick to it."

"All right. I got it."

"And, Belle?"

"Yes?"

"Be careful."

"I will. I'll call you when the deed is done," Belle said and disconnected the phone.

She checked herself one last time in the mirror before leaving the dressing room. The first stop she made was at the bar for a bottle of champagne, a corkscrew, and two glasses. She kept a pleasant smile on her face as she maneuvered her way through the heavy crowd of men. They all seemed to be having the time of their lives. Belle wondered what they would do with themselves when the Bliss Lounge ceased to exist. Maybe they would find a new club to go to, or maybe their need for a place like that would die with the lounge. There was only one way to see.

Belle's heart almost thumped out of her chest when she got to the golden office door. She'd been around Gene many times before, but now that she knew he was the man who killed her parents, it was different. At a time like that she wished she had one of Drip's magical pills to take the edge off. Belle counted to five twice before she mustered up the courage to put her fist to the door.

Knock! Knock!

"Who is that?"

"Me. Lady Beauty," she said.

Within seconds the door swung open wide, and Gene stood there wearing a big smile. "You must have read my mind. I was just about to send for you," he said and moved out of the way so she could enter.

"You know what they say about great minds," she said and stepped past him.

He shut the door behind her, and she couldn't help but feel like a zebra locked inside a room with a tiger. Placing his hands on the small of her back, Gene leaned in and kissed her on the cheek. The place where his lips touched her skin seemed like it started to crawl, and she tried her best to hold the smile on her face. What she really wanted to do was gag.

"What's this you have here?" he asked, looking at her hands.

Suddenly she remembered the champagne she brought. "Just a little something for the two of us to enjoy," she said to him. "Do you mind if I pour it for us?"

"No, be my guest," he said and let her go over to a table he had at the side of his office.

She set the glasses down gently before opening the bottle of bubbly. After she poured the drinks, she used her peripheral vision to make sure he could not see what she was doing, and then she quietly unzipped her fanny pack. From it, she pulled out a small ketamine pill to drop in one of the glasses.

"I'm glad you came up here," Gene's voice said from right behind her, startling her into dropping the pill in one of the glasses.

She couldn't tell which glass the pill went in because of the bubbles, and she began to panic. Gene grabbed one of the glasses without waiting for Belle to hand it to him. With a shaky hand, she picked up the remaining glass and faced him. She couldn't believe that had just happened. All she could do was hope that the glass he had chosen was the one with the drug in it.

"And why is that?" she asked, trying to buy herself some time.

"I wanted to discuss something with you, something important."

"And that is?"

"You."

"Me?" she said and faked a giggle. "What about me?"

"I would be lying to you, Lady Beauty, if I said seeing all of those men ogling over you didn't do something nasty to my spirit. I almost hate it."

"Oh?"

"See, I've never felt an infatuation like this before. It's something that I'm not used to."

"That's hard to believe, being that you're surrounded by so many pretty women at all times."

"Yet none of them are as breathtaking as you," he said to her. "Which is why I have to fire you."

"Fire me? But why?"

"Because I need you for a far bigger title. Lady Beauty, I want you to be my wife."

"Your wife?" Belle exclaimed a little louder than she wanted to.

"I know it's sudden, and you might feel that you don't know me at all. But I assure you that I will keep you very happy. You'll have everything you need and more. And the best part is that you'll never have to work another day in your life."

Belle truly couldn't believe the nerve of him. He was even worse than she believed. He had robbed her of everything that had given her happiness yet stood before her claiming that he could make her happy. It took about all of her self-control to not grab the bottle of champagne and crash it on his temple. However, her smile dropped, and there was no way of getting it back on her face. She just stood there, staring incredulously up at him.

"Well, uh, I . . . I'm flattered," she forced out.

"Then what do you say?" he asked her and pulled a small box from his pocket. "Will you do me the honor of becoming the most important lady in my life?"

He opened it and flashed the biggest diamond Belle had ever seen in her life. It was so beautiful, something that Gene was incapable of being or deserving. *How dare he?* Still, Belle needed to buy herself some time. Kidd said that if he didn't hear from her within fifteen minutes of her being alone with Gene, he was going to come get her. Her thoughts were going a mile a minute in her brain, but she knew there was only one thing to do.

"Yes," she said.

"Yes?" he asked. Even he was shocked by her answer.

"Yes," she repeated. "Of course I'll marry you, Gene. You've done so much for me and have been so kind to me. If this will ease your mind, then so be it."

He took her hand in his and slid the big rock on her finger. It was a perfect fit, and even she had to admit how good it looked on her delicate hand. He raised his glass in the air, and she did the same.

"To new beginnings. May our worlds collide in more ways than just one!" he said, looking her dead in the eyes. "Drink!"

His word came out as a demand, and Belle was the ant caught under the magnifying glass. He downed his drink, and if she didn't, he would know something was up. She prayed that his cup was the one with the pill in it, and she took a big gulp of her drink. After she swallowed, he took the glass from her and set both down by the champagne bottle.

"Now," he said, running a finger down her collarbone, "how about we make things more official?"

As his finger dropped to her breasts, Belle started to feel herself get lightheaded.

Shit. I drank the wrong glass! she thought, but she was growing too woozy to panic. The pill worked fast, and its effects were strong even though she hadn't drunk all of the liquid. She suddenly lost her balance in her tall stilettos and fell into Gene, giving him the notion that she wanted him.

"Oh, you're the aggressive type I see," he said and lifted her up. His hand rubbed against her bare vagina lips. "No panties. I like it. Let's have some fun, shall we?"

***

Kidd stood at the bottom of the staircase that led up to Gene's office, waiting impatiently for word from Belle. He'd relieved the security guard who had been watching the staircase and took his place. It had been almost ten minutes, and he still didn't have a call or text from her. He wondered what the hell was going on up there.

"What are you doing?" Aria's voice said as she came from out of nowhere.

"What does it look like I'm doin'?" he snapped. He noticed that she had a bottle of vodka in her hand.

"What happened to Larry?" she asked, speaking about the previous security guard.

"I told him I would take over for him for a little while. I'm waiting for Gene anyways."

"Liar," Aria said. "I saw Belle go up there not too long ago. That's who you're really waiting for."

"Why does it matter to you?"

"Because if you are waiting for her, you're too late." Her words alarmed him at first, but then she continued. "Whatever you hoped could be between you is no more. Gene plans on marrying her. That bastard."

"He plans on doing what?"

"He plans on making Belle his wife," she said and took a drink straight from the bottle. "After everything I've done for him. And he wants to marry a bitch we found on the street."

"Aria, you're drunk," Kidd said, noticing the slur in her speech. "Go back with the other girls."

"Fuck that," Aria said. "Those motherfuckers are going to hear from me!"

Kidd didn't have time to grab her before she shot up the stairs. He ran after her, but she was moving so fast in her stilettos that he kept grabbing air.

"Gene!" she yelled. "Gene! You slimy motherfucker!"

When she got to the golden door, she opened the door and pushed it wide. Kidd was right on her heels, but he stopped in his tracks once he saw what was going on in the office. Gene had knocked everything off of his desk and was positioning himself to sexually penetrate a barely conscious Belle.

"Ay, man, what the fuck?" Kidd said. "First you kill her family, and now you rape her?"

"What are you doing in here? Where's Larry?" Gene asked, buttoning his pants back up.

"Get the fuck away from her," Kidd barked and pulled his gun out. "If you so much as touch her, I'll blow your head from your shoulders."

"I can touch my fiancée if I please," Gene said simply and didn't budge. "Now get out of my office."

"Fiancée!" Aria exclaimed. When she saw the ring on Belle's finger, she launched the bottle of vodka at Gene. It missed his head by a few centimeters. "After everything I've done for you?"

In a dash, she was on Gene like white on rice, hitting him with closed fists wherever they would land. Her screams were those of a broken-hearted woman, and the liquor in her system only amplified her emotions. Aria was getting him so good that he had cowered over. She was in the middle of another punch attack when the shots rang out.

Bang! Bang! Bang!

"Uh," she groaned in pain and stumbled back, holding her stomach.

Blood was seeping through her fingers, and there was a look of shock on her face. While she was busy trying to beat some sense into him, she hadn't even seen that he'd bent down to get the gun taped under his desktop.

"You shot me. Why?" she asked, coughing up more blood.

"Every bitch is replaceable," Gene said to her as she dropped to the ground. "Even you."

"Aria," Belle whispered from on top of the desk and reached for her, but it was too late for her friend.

Gene turned his gun to Belle and averted his eyes to his nephew. "Drop that gun, little nigga," he said. "I know she's your soft spot. By the time you can let one off at me, I'd have already put two in her skull."

Kidd hesitated, but when Gene cocked his gun, Kidd dropped his weapon. But that didn't mean his mouth didn't work.

"I know what you did to my mother," Kidd spat. "I know you set her up to take the fall for you."

"I knew letting you talk to that bitch was a bad idea."

"Damn, you really don't give a fuck about women. Not even your own sister. You had me hatin' my own mother!"

"What can I say? You do what you have to do in business." Gene shrugged. Kidd started toward him, but Gene wagged a finger. "Ah, ah, ah. Stop it or she dies."

"You aren't gon' kill her," Kidd said.

"And what makes you so sure of that?"

"Because you still need her, don't you? That's why you want to marry her. You can't kill her."

"All right, you called my bluff," Gene said and pointed the gun at him. "I can't kill her, you're right. If you knew that, it was dumb of you to drop your gun and leave yourself defenseless. Because I can kill you."

"You could. But you won't. Because you'll be dead before you can even squeeze the trigger."

"And who's going to kill me?" Gene laughed scornfully. "You?"

"Nah. Somebody else deserves your soul more than me."

On Kidd's last word, Aria lifted up and aimed the gun that Kidd had dropped next to her at Gene's head. She tugged the trigger one time and sent a bullet right through the middle of Gene's forehead. The power of the shot snapped his head back, and his eyes were wide open, frozen in shock. Aria had used to rest of her energy to send him to hell, and his body falling to the floor was the last thing she saw before she too left the land of the living.

Kidd left his gun in her hand, knowing that the police would need it as evidence when he called and reported the double homicide. He stepped over Aria's body and scooped Belle up in his arms. She was going in and out of consciousness. He kissed her forehead as he carried her out of the office and out of that lounge. He swore to himself that she would never step foot in that place again.

Beep. Beep.

The distant yet constant sound of the beeping was what brought Belle to open her eyes. They fluttered slightly, and she tried to make sense of her surroundings. She was in some sort of bed, which wasn't the most comfortable, she might add. And that annoying beeping, where was it coming from?

"Welcome back," a familiar voice said.

Whipping her head, she smiled when she saw Kidd's face not too far from her. He looked restless, like he'd been up all night.

"Where am I?"

"The hospital," he told her. "Apparently you slipped yourself a date-rape drug."

"Oh, my God," she said weakly. "I messed up. The pill slipped, and I didn't know which glass it went in."

"It's all right. Everything worked out."

"Is it . . . is it over?"

"Yes," Kidd said. "How much do you remember after you drank from the wrong glass?"

"I remember . . ." Belle said and tried to force her memories back. "I remember you coming in. But you weren't alone. You were with . . . Oh, my God. Aria. Is she—"

"Dead? Yes."

"No." Belle shook her head violently and tried to hold back the tears. "No."

"Hey," Kidd said and grabbed her hand. "It's all right."

She nodded and swallowed the large lump in her throat. She wished that the vision she had of Aria getting shot by Gene was just a nightmare. But it wasn't. Aria had fallen victim to the life that had saved her, like so many others before her. It wrenched Belle's heart terribly. Was living even worth it after dealing with so much loss?

"I can't believe how much my life has spiraled in such a short amount of time. I don't have any family left."

"You have me," Kidd said. "I'm your family now. And I ain't goin' nowhere no time soon."

"Promise?"

"Word as bond."

"So, what now?"

"Now we move on with our lives. They found Gene's and Aria's bodies this mornin'. The police are rulin' it as a domestic dispute between lovers."

"It's the truth."

"Yeah. He deserved it. . . ." Kidd's voice trailed off.

"What about the Bliss Lounge?"

"I haven't decided what I'm gon' do with it yet. I'll figure it out in due time. But first, there's something else I need to do."

Kidd kissed Belle's knuckles as she gazed at him. He truly did believe that fate had brought them together. He didn't know why or what the future held in store for him. What he did know was that wherever he was supposed to be, he was sure it was with her. Belle. The beauty to his beast.

Epilogue

Bzzz!

The sound of the prison door buzzing was one that Gia would not miss. Words couldn't express how happy she was to be saying goodbye to the terrible place she had called home for the past ten years. She'd had faith that her son would do it, and he did. He had not only defeated Gene but also turned the Bliss Lounge into a regular gentlemen's club called the Rose Room. That way, all of the girls there would still be employed. There were no more contracts, and no more blood would be spilled, not as much anyway.

She had hated having to put on him the burden of taking out the trash, but there was nobody else who could have handled an evil man like Gene. After all, Kidd learned everything he knew from his uncle. The world being rid of a man like Gene Hightower had been the icing on the cake for Gia, but her son did her one better.

When Gene died, Kidd used a few of his files to blackmail the governor and prosecutor on Gia's case. Whatever he had on them was enough for them to file a motion to release Gia immediately. When she found out, she dropped down to her knees and cried tears of joy. She thought that she'd spend the rest of her days trapped by those jail walls.

On her way out, she was given a bag filled with the things she'd come in with. In it were some clothes that didn't fit, some shoes she didn't want, a hair clip, and a locket. The only thing she removed from the bag was the locket. Inside it was a picture of her son's sweet face when he was just 8 years old. It was her favorite picture of him because he had a snaggletooth. She smiled when she saw it and kissed it before placing it around her neck.

"You're a free woman, Gia," the female guard said to her as they walked her to the doors she would be exiting through. "How does it feel?"

"What do you mean, how does it feel?" Gia asked with a joyous laugh. "I'm free!"

"Just don't do anything that will land you back here."

"Trust me, I won't," Gia said. "I missed out on so much time with my son. All I want to do is make up for lost time."

"Sounds like a good plan," the guard said and opened one of the double doors for her. "This is where I say goodbye and good luck!"

The bright sun hit Gia in the face, and she welcomed it. She walked out of the door and through the prison gates feeling like a whole new woman. Once she was in the parking lot, she used her hand as a visor and searched around for a familiar face. Kidd said that he would be there to pick her up. She hoped that he didn't forget about her.

"Mama!" she heard a deep voice call from behind her.

Her heart dropped to her stomach, but in a happy way, when she turned around and saw the face of her Andrew. He was standing by a Range Rover and wearing a nice white collared shirt with the top buttons undone. The navy blue pants he wore stopped right above his ankles, and the loafers on his feet were so white that the ground should have felt graced by their presence. He was muscular and more handsome than she ever dreamed he would be. The young boy she'd left was a grown man now, and her heart was so elated. Her feet started toward him, and before she knew it, she was running. He started running too, and when they finally met, she jumped into his arms. She clung to him and sobbed harder than she ever thought she could, kissing him all over his face.

"My son! Oh, my son! I'm so sorry! I love you so much!" she said over and over. When she finally got the strength to pull away, she looked in his face and saw that he too was crying.

"Let's go home," he said, looking down at her.

"I'm living with you?"

"Hell yeah!" Kidd said, linking his arm with hers and walking her to the car. "I'm not letting you out of my sight for a long time to come. I found the perfect house for all of us."

"That's all right with me," Gia told him. "Wait, who's all of us?"

As soon as the question was out of her mouth, the passenger door opened, and a young woman got out. She was wearing a long off-white maxi dress and had long hair that she had in a neat ponytail to the back of her head. Gia was hit with a blast from the past when she looked into her face.

"Mama, I'd like to introduce you to somebody. This is Belle. Belle Dubois," Kidd said, holding his hand out for Belle to come closer.

Gia's hands shot to her mouth, and more tears flooded from her eyes. Belle was even more lovely on the eyes than her mother had been, and Gia couldn't stop staring.

"Hi," Belle said to her and gave a little wave. She was shocked when Gia returned it with an embrace. "Oh!"

Belle returned the hug and held Gia tightly like she too needed the love. Gia released her and placed a hand on her flawless cheek. Her heart was so filled with joy that she feared it might explode.

"Let's get out of here before these crackers try to take me back," Gia said and headed for the car.

"Yes!" Belle said and held the passenger door open for her. "We have a few things in store for you today. The world has changed a lot since you've been away. Our first stop, however, is shopping of course!"

"Shopping?" Gia said and got in the car.

"Yes, shoppin'!" Kidd said. "I gotta get my mama right. Luella is gon' meet us at the mall, and I'ma give you a few dollars to play around with."

Belle hopped in the driver's seat, and Kidd got in the back. When Belle pulled away from the prison and started the long drive back home, Kidd reached up and grabbed his mother's hand as if he were afraid that she would disappear at any second. Gia turned to face him and looked fondly into his eyes.

"I'm so proud of the man you've become," she told him. "I know it wasn't easy, growing up without me around. But you did it, and you did well for yourself. You, my dear boy, are everything I ever thought you would be and more."

"I love you," Kidd told her.

"And I love you ten times more."

The End